A SLIGHT CURVE

A. MOLOTKOV

Paperback ISBN: 978-1-963869-17-0
eBook ISBN: 978-1-963869-18-7

"...a human being had died. It did not matter. Thousands of people died every moment. There were statistics about it. It did not matter. For the one individual, however, it meant everything and was more important than the still revolving world."

Erich Maria Remarque, from *Arch of Triumph*

CHAPTER ONE

With growing concern, Ruth watched a white car headed toward her on the highway below. Instead of following the highway's slight curve, the car kept going straight. Ruth couldn't see the driver through the windshield's glare.

She stood on a hill over the highway, her hands on her hips, her long hair horizontal in the wind. The ocean's mass danced in shades of gray beyond the rows of cars parked at the Cliff House. Its elegant white pavilion, home to a small museum and a restaurant, stood sharp against the backdrop of the waves.

Brakes screeched—too late—the truck was upon the white car, then over it, subsuming the small thing with its massive body. The crunch of metal and the scream of breaking glass mixed in Ruth's ears. Her nails dug into her palms. She couldn't breathe. Gigantic tomatoes painted on the truck loomed, obscenely red. The car lay on its back, one of the wheels still spinning. Ruth shivered, managed a short breath. She could not accept this, not so soon after her father's passing. But it had happened, she could not un-see it.

The air rising from the crash smelled offensive, poisoned. Burning plastic with its petroleum core—and something else. Rubber. Ruth imagined a rubber molecule, so firm in its resolve, yet flexible—elongated like a lifetime, running away from itself. She forced herself to breathe.

The driver stepped out of the cab of his truck, looking stunned. Moving slowly, he and several pedestrians reached the white car at the same time. A young man in a green coat knelt next to the driver's side. He leaned over and peered inside for an endless time. He turned back toward the others and shook his head.

Ruth was crying: for whoever was in the white car, for herself, for Dad, who had died a week earlier. *All this death—it's too much.* She felt out of place up on the hill—an observer, too far, entirely too far from everything. Irrelevant, unable to help. The people in the scene below seemed to move in slow motion as if the new balance of life and death was beginning to establish itself. She *needed* to be down there.

A barely visible path led down the slope, the soil loose under her feet. Thorns from small bushes nipped at her ankles. She slipped on a rock and almost lost her balance.

The chemical stench increased as the smoke spread. An ambulance had arrived, followed by the police. A fire truck rested at an angle across both lanes. The backs of a growing crowd cut off the rest of Ruth's view. By getting closer, she had distanced herself. She glanced at the spot on the hill where she had stood, the earth's jagged edge against a deceptively blue sky.

"What's happening? What's happening?" she asked various strangers. But they were trying to answer that question for themselves. Two long lines of waiting cars were building up.

A blonde kid around twelve made his way out of the crowd with an occasional "I'm sorry." Despite the chilly day and the strong wind from the ocean, he wore no coat, just a light yellow T-shirt.

"Hey." Ruth stopped him. "Who was it?"

"This lady." The kid sounded matter-of-fact. "I think she's dead."

"What lady?" Ruth's question didn't make sense; she knew that the moment she asked it.

"I don't know." The kid shrugged. "Just some lady."

Through the shifting bodies, Ruth caught an occasional glimpse of the white car. The medics were loading their stretcher into a black van, their faces gloomy, unengaged. The figure on the stretcher was covered in white. Ruth's red jacket was the wrong color, like that gigantic tomato on the truck. Somehow, she felt involved in the accident. Tears streamed down her cheeks.

The ambulance drove off without sirens or lights, and all at once, the observers' interest waned. They began to disperse. Ruth hesitated. The white car remained in place, no longer smoking. A tow truck had arrived. The ocean was gray, indifferent. The police hung around, consulting and taking pictures. Ruth was shivering. She had to get home.

The following day, Ruth lay on the couch, her mind meandering. Through the window, glimpses of blue among the branches looked too real.

Ruth had been unaccustomed to death until recently, when its empty space became a haunting reality. Death made sense in biological terms, which were chemical terms—but witnessing someone's removal from life was a different thing. Something about the accident stuck with her as an unfinished story. *The lady in the car, how old was she?* Ruth opened her laptop and searched for "accident on Great Highway." Yesterday's news hadn't made it to the press yet.

Maybe the driver got distracted by a cup of coffee? What if the plastic lid was about to fall off, and holding it in place stole that extra second of attention? Perhaps she died with coffee as the last taste in her mouth? Not such a bad way to go.

Ruth stretched out, the couch fabric rough under her legs. The room was white, a perfect background for brighter things. The furniture, cheap but functional, all she could afford for now. Chemists didn't make as much as lawyers or doctors.

The thing the kid had said kept replaying in her mind. *Just some lady.*

Ruth was dozing off. The white car glistened in the moonlight, the wrong kind of glisten. The hands on the wheel were pale, not Ruth's hands. Then she woke up. The sun had surrendered control of the window. Ruth must have slept a few hours.

The laptop was her first thought. She refreshed the news website. There it was.

Driver Dead in a Great Highway Accident.

Ruth clicked.

Ulrike Schumacher, 34, died in a traffic accident when she apparently lost control of her vehicle while driving North on The Great Highway, within San Francisco city limits. She was declared dead at the scene at 5:34 p.m.

Ulrike. Ulrike Schumacher. Ruth teared up, rereading. There was no picture. Ruth closed her eyes to imagine.

CHAPTER TWO

Ulrike rolls up the car windows. Time to head home. The city is gray, unassuming. This section of Mission Street buzzes with a multicultural vibe, so different from her childhood of white faces. She loves this mélange of races and lifestyles. Colors and designs dance before her eyes, and her mind enjoys the experience. On Van Ness, she begins to feel sleepy and must focus for the remaining five minutes as she drives to her lovely and too-expensive Nob Hill apartment.

Peter is already home. He is preoccupied like an intelligent hedgehog. Typical. Even as he comes out to the foyer to welcome her, he wears that absent, worried look. Ulrike doesn't have the energy to break through Peter's lack of engagement. A few words will suffice. They kiss briefly. *He does look great in a T-shirt and a pair of jeans.* She smiles.

She finds Black men irresistible. In her youth, their images were mysterious and obscure, relegated to films and magazines. Girls in her class used to fantasize about them. And now, this beautiful man is in her life. Still, something inside her is dissatisfied, lacking— what? Something she doesn't have a name for.

They walk into the living room. Ulrike parks her purse on the couch and stretches, happy to be home for the rest of the evening. Just now, the clouds dwell elsewhere; light enters the windows in a pleasant way. The red curtains are pulled apart, trembling in the wind. Sounds from the street drift softly in. She loves the high ceilings, this airy design choice. Her friend Brigita, an architect, has praised California styles.

If only Ulrike could allow herself to linger with these pleasant thoughts—but today's experience with a client reminds her that life is shitless shit, and she'd better get used to it.

"How was your day?" she asks perfunctorily as Peter lingers.

"Good. Good." Peter's thoughts are still on something else. "And you?" he adds after a long pause.

He sits astride one of the white dining room chairs, his muscular arms embracing the back.

"So-so. I lost that boutique website project. That lady is such a mistake of nature."

"Why? What happened?"

I was robbed of something, a part of my dignity, even though I hadn't done much, and the 50% down payment is mine to keep. Ulrike could recount every detail, but it would be excessive, tiresome.

"She's a passive-aggressive bitch. She was spoiling for a fight— going on and on about the deadline. I got backed up but still had time to complete the job. I have a contract. Could take her to small claims court for the remaining 750 bucks. Just don't know if it's worth it."

"It's not fair that she fired you." Peter's eyes are supportive, but something about it bothers Ulrike as if nothing at all will do today. She is mad at herself. Every client's obsessions take time, more time than originally anticipated. *I'm terrible at planning.* Something in her wants to tell Peter to be critical, to make it more difficult for her to get away without acknowledging her own share of responsibility. But she can't find the right words.

"No," she says instead. "Come on, give me a hug."

Ulrike wraps her arms around him, feels his broad shoulders. He is so warm and dear in her arms, his smell so familiar.

1983, DRESDEN, EAST GERMANY

The sun slaps her on the face, a massive wave of warmth. The school's heavy brown door closes behind her with that whoosh Ulrike loves so much, the final sound of her school day. Her red *Thälmann Pioneer* necktie waves in the wind. Brigita stands next to her, her second self. There is little the two girls disagree on. Brigita is thin, brittle, and smaller than most girls their age. Her red tie is enormous hanging from her neck.

Ulrike considers dispensing with the tie, but doing so on the school's porch could be considered provocative. She'll have to wait a few more minutes. The red thing is choking her in this heat. She won't miss it when she joins *Freie Deutsche Jugend* later this year. At official events, Free German Youth wear blue shorts—a nauseating blue, but at least no red tie. One more reason to celebrate the age of fourteen.

Kids scatter to their afternoon goals, their yells disappearing down elegant Dresden streets. Ulrike looks forward to lunch, to reading, to doing something with Brigita. Both girls are silent. They enjoy this part, the school's emptying out, the silence that eventually emerges from chaos. They linger at the top of the stairs.

"Ulrike Schumacher?" A low male voice.

Right in front of the school building is a beige, nondescript Moskvitch made by the stupid Russians in their stupid USSR. It's parked with its wrong side to the curb as if it had arrived here in defiance of traffic rules. The man behind the wheel stares at her, leaving no doubt that he owns the firm, deep voice she heard. Ulrike's legs turn rubbery as the girls walk toward the car.

"My name is Doctor Vogel."

The man is tall and elderly, his hair gray, his face thin and inexpressive. He wears a heavy blue overcoat inappropriate for the sweltering day. He doesn't seem the least bit uncomfortable, sprawled there in the driver's seat with a fat brown folder resting against the steering wheel.

"Doctor?" The question just comes out. Nothing signals medicine in the man's appearance. There's something wrong with this situation, but Ulrike can't quite tell what. *How does he know my name?*

"A Doctor of Sciences. Can we talk in private?"

What sciences? she wants to ask. *Why in private?*

Then it strikes her.

He's a Stasi.

Her body tightens. How dumb not to get it right away. She'd never had an encounter, just heard of them. Everyone has.

Why me?

What am I supposed to do?

Should I run?

She looks over at Brigita, who seems utterly puzzled. A second later, Brigita's mouth opens, her face tenses. She, too, understands.

"Go home," Ulrike instructs. "I'll call you later."

The Stasi wants her, not Brigita.

Why me?

"Okay." Brigita tries to smile, but her face is more a grimace. Still, she lingers.

Ulrike waves goodbye, awkwardly, not the way the two girls have ever used. Brigita finally complies, begins walking away. She keeps turning to look. Ulrike wishes for a grownup on her side just now, not another schoolgirl like Brigita. Someone who would protect her, not someone she has to protect. This is unfamiliar territory, scary and unpredictable. She feels it in her mouth—a metallic taste. *My life is over.*

As if reading her thoughts, the man produces his green *Ministerium für Staatssicherheit* card. "Fräulein Schumacher, would you please take a ride with me?" Vogel gestures toward the passenger seat.

Brigita has stopped half a block down, watching, but Vogel doesn't seem to care. He doesn't seem to care about anything at all. Ulrike knows she is not supposed to get into the cars of strange men, but this is different. She can't exactly say no. No one has provided instructions on what to do when a Stasi asked her into his car.

Ulrike's wooden legs carry her around the vehicle. She struggles with the unfamiliar door handle. Her uncle's Trabant is different. Vogel offers no help, doesn't even turn her way.

She masters it after many awkward seconds. As she gets in, the man's face remains vacant, directed elsewhere. His hands in black leather gloves are stuck to the steering wheel. The beige leather seat under her feels firm yet slippery, as if too many poor souls had spilled their fears on it. She runs her hand along it. It's not the seat that's slippery—it's her sweaty hand.

Is this my file he's looking at?

"Where..." Ulrike's clears her throat. "Where are we going?"

"A beautiful day, isn't it?" Briefly, Vogel turns his head toward her—not all the way, not exactly facing her, just acknowledging a presence. "The afternoon is only beginning. Do you have a lot of homework?"

"Homework?"

Why is he asking this? She feels small, vulnerable. Her fists are tight in her lap, fingers pressing into the palms so hard the nails nearly puncture the skin.

"You know, I never did my homework when I was at school. Would you believe that? Never could force myself to sit down and study. Imagine that. Always did better at sports, not thinking." Vogel pauses and turns over a couple of pages in his folder. "I was a simple kid. Now it's different. This job takes more thinking than one would expect. Do you like thinking?"

Is that a trick question?

"Thinking?" Ulrike mumbles.

"Some people like it too much."

"Where are we going?" Ulrike repeats.

"Our office, just a few blocks from here. Don't worry; I'll drive you back when we're done."

"Thank you." She is scared shitless, but she might as well be polite.

Ulrike looks out the window to avoid the Stasi even in her peripheral vision. She knows to say as little as possible without appearing uncooperative.

Is it something stupid I blabbed at a party? Is this about that Erich Honecker on Leonid Brezhnev lip kiss from a couple of years ago? A kiss that would be erotic if it weren't so pathetic. In the photographs, the two stand surrounded by a group of embarrassed high-ranking USSR and GDR officials averting their eyes. The kiss jokes are commonplace, almost allowed—but not in the literal sense.

Vogel parks by a four-story residential building on a side street. *Not far from my apartment. I may have walked here before.* She seems to remember the way the dark courtyard hides from view, accessible only via a small tunnel through the building's facade. But there are many such places in Dresden.

Vogel walks across the front of the car and opens the door for her, like some fake gentleman. And there they are, headed into a secluded space where anything could happen. The neighborhood is quiet.

Will I see my family again?

Will they let me call them?

She's nauseated. *Shit! Throwing up in front of the Stasi would be the worst.* She forces herself to breathe, just breathe. Vogel leads her up a flight of stairs and unlocks what looks like a typical apartment. The lights are on; voices in the background. Ulrike sighs in relief.

"Over here." Vogel gestures toward a door.

The room is dark, the curtains drawn against the world. Vogel flips the switch. Light green wallpaper covers the walls. A simple brown desk with a massive office chair leaves room for three elegant Czechoslovakian chairs upholstered in dark blue, too well-made for this place. Vogel drops into his own massive seat. Honecker's portrait hovers over his desk. East Germany's dictator looks friendly and imminently more photogenic in his younger years than many other socialist villains.

What if this Vogel can read my facial expression? Could I incriminate myself just by acting worried? Should I sit? She waits, hovers next to the chairs. Vogel is in no rush to make her comfortable.

A 1977 poster fades on the wall to her right, Lenin's stern white face infused with red—a head floating in a tub of blood. On Lenin's right eyebrow perch enthusiastic men in uniforms, their weapons pointed at enemies of socialism outside the frame. Over the years, the red has become orange, but the expression on Lenin's face remains ominous—you wouldn't want to meet a man like that on a narrow forest path. Ulrike has seen this poster hundreds of times before. It's the only familiar thing in the room. 60. *Jahrestag Der Grossen Sozialistischen Oktoberrevolution* (60 Years of the Great October Revolution), explain the white letters at the bottom.

A narrow bookcase with official literature sits next to the window. *What about this apartment's former inhabitants?*

Probably arrested by the Stasi.

"Have a seat." Vogel finally offers.

With a pen between his fingers, he points vaguely in the direction of the empty chairs. The fat folder he had in the car now lies open on the desk between them. *Is this my file?* Ulrike wonders again with growing dread. *Is this my life?*

"Let's get down to business." Vogel stares right into her eyes this time. "Your uncle has agreed to cooperate. If you help us, everyone will be better off. The country will take care of you and your family. But if you end up being a liar—well, then it's a different matter."

CHAPTER THREE

2003

Ruth opened her eyes. Her room was real and solid around her. The evening had settled outside.

"Ms. Schumacher was survived by her husband, Peter Litmanowic," the article had read. *An odd name, Litmanowic.* The computer screen shone at Ruth, with the power, the lure of immense, unimaginable information at her fingertips. Just a few seconds of waiting, and numerous results came up. The top one read,

SF Environment Staff | sfenvironment.org - Our Home.
Our ...

She clicked—and there he was, mid-page amid green. Energy & Climate Program Manager. A picture next to it. A Black guy, good-looking. The dead woman's husband, with his name linked to an email address and his phone number right there, on the page.

Ruth clicked the email link.

The blank space of an empty message loomed. This was too easy—the way things happen in films, not in real life. She started writing.

Dear Peter,

You don't know me, but

After some deliberation, Ruth deleted the second line.

Dear Peter,

I realize this is a tragic time for you, and you don't even know me. But I had to write to tell you that I was there when your wife died. I saw it happen. I'm not sure if I can contribute anything to what you already know. Still, I wanted to tell you that I was there, and I was terrified and so sad for her. I've felt sick ever since. I know it's of no help to you. I'm not sure why I'm writing. Maybe just to let you know that someone saw the whole thing. That's all. Forgive me.

Ruth reread the last part. She reread the entire email once more. She added:

What I'm trying to say is that I watched her car, and it was there, just fine, and then it went off course. I don't know why. The highway curves in that spot. Anyway, I don't mean to intrude. If this email is of no interest to you, please ignore it.

Ruth reread it again and saved it, for now. She was tired. She got up to pour herself some red wine. The color was lovely through the glass.

* * *

Ruth opened her eyes. How long had she slept? Morning had invaded, fresh and generous with light. Hours must have passed.

She flipped her laptop open, stared a while at the black screen. Pressed a button to bring the screen alive.

Her rambling email was as bad and as good as any such attempt could ever be.

She pressed *Send*.

* * *

11 am; too early to eat. Ruth ordered a coffee as she waited for her mother. They often met here at TJ's, just around the corner from Ruth's apartment. Linda liked to visit the oceanfront.

The place was small, efficient, and rather generic. It served decent coffee, burgers, and all kinds of high-calorie goodies. With their iron legs and laminate tops, the tables were functional and sufficient, if not particularly elegant. Not everything had to be perfect every time. The green walls were as predictable as walls could be.

Her mother came in, looking around conspicuously as if it took a long deliberation to spot her daughter among the two or three people present. Linda wore an elegant blue dress, her hair up in a bun. Her broad face remained good-looking, revealing former powers over men, which, as far as Ruth knew, had misfired in her parents' marriage.

Linda was as thin now as she'd ever been in Ruth's memory. Ruth rose to hug her. Her mother's shoulders felt skeletal.

"Mother, how are you? I'm so worried about you."

16

"I'm okay, dear. Thank you."

They sat down. The owner, Fred, a large guy with a nonde-script face, already knew what her mother wanted: a coffee and a jelly donut.

"You know, I keep imagining him there, on the rails." Ruth stared intensely into her mother's eyes, trying to connect. "The body was...you know, you saw it."

"Yes." Linda looked out the window as if engaged in the antics of the empty street. "There's no need to dwell on that part, dear."

"What was he doing in El Cerrito, on a workday?"

Linda remained silent. This trick always worked to infuriate her daughter.

"What, you're just going to ignore my question?"

"I'm not interested," Linda said. "The man is gone. It's just like him, to do something terrible like that and disappear. This whole thing may hurt us if we keep pushing and pushing against it."

The statement made no logical sense—or too much sense. Ruth replied with a stare, trying to infuse it with a mountain of disdain so vast it would obliterate Linda's profound indifference.

It didn't work; Linda wasn't making eye contact.

"*It's just like him?* What do you mean, Mother?"

"In a manner of speaking, darling. In a manner of speaking. I miss him every bit as much as you do—hell, more. We've spent our lives together." Briefly, Linda's well-maintained round face with its dimples bore the expression of the most profound loss—then she mastered it again.

"You two used to bicker a lot," Ruth said. "Do you remember?"

"We were young. We disagreed sometimes, that's true. People do that."

"Don't you want to find out what happened? He may have been killed, for god sake. I can't believe you don't care."

Linda employed a large sip of coffee to facilitate a dramatic pause. "What's there to find out? It was an accident. Lesley must have gone to El Cerrito for business or something. There must be a reason."

"He didn't even show up at work that day." Ruth was annoyed. "How could it be for business?"

"I don't know *any* of the answers." Linda was her reasonable, logical persona. "And one of the things life has taught me is not to ask too many questions."

"You're terrible, Mother. I don't want to talk about it anymore. I have to go."

Ruth placed a five-dollar bill next to her saucer. Her coffee was only halfway consumed. Her mother's donut too, its insides glistening with their sticky invitation.

Linda just stared with an ambiguous half-smile. Ruth walked out without another word.

1983

Still in its cardboard box, a large pepperoni pizza, their favorite, steamed in the center of the round dining room table. Ruth pulled a second slice from the box, placing it on an elegant plate of Russian china her mother had inherited from her parents. Exquisitely curved blue patterns ran around the plate's edges, connecting in the center. The pizza triangle, surrounded by these lines, could be a work of art.

"Dad, you work in loans, right?"

"That's right, dear."

Mom had claimed one of her nights away from family duty, withdrawing to the dark bedroom to lie down and feel miserable. It was dinner for two. Ruth preferred this. Dad at least engaged in conversation; Mom—she was elsewhere most of the time. At fourteen, being listened to mattered.

"Why do you travel so much? Can't you discuss these loans over the phone?"

Dad refused to hold a pizza slice in his hand, insisting on a fork and a knife instead. He carefully placed the piece he'd cut off in his mouth and chewed on it for a few seconds before speaking.

"I travel for meetings with other managers, to discuss our work. Most of the time there are many people in the meeting. It would be awkward over the phone. Why are you so interested?" He smiled.

"I just want to know more about you. What kind of improvements do you make?"

Ruth needed to grasp how things clicked into place. Her mind worked that way, forever puzzling over people, events, and objects —until she understood or discovered she'd need to study more to understand.

"It's all about finances. It's difficult to explain without some accounting basics."

"If I'm old enough to understand chemistry, I must be old enough to understand accounting."

Just over a year ago, she'd asked for a chemistry kit for a birthday present. She was hooked.

"Yes, Ruthie. But it would make for a long story, to explain it all from the start." Under his awkward half-smile, Ruth sensed genuine discomfort. He really didn't want to talk about this.

She wished Dad would ask her about her opinions, her life. But his thoughts always seemed to hover elsewhere, unless directly solicited by a question. She had to volunteer information if she wanted to be noticed.

Ruth took a bite. The pizza was better than she'd remembered. She rediscovered the taste each time they ordered from Tony's. *What makes the smell so irresistible? What ensures the taste? It's chemistry. Everything is. Can a chemist produce a pizza smell without a pizza?*

"Dad, how did you even get into finances?"

"You and I seem to share an interest in numbers. Everyone needs people who are good with them. My first job happened to be in banking—it was okay, better than most. I just stayed with it."

Ruth couldn't trace back the beginnings of her mental process, her preferences as she understood them now. Certain things were interesting—others, not so much. What was that notion, *interesting?* It felt like an engagement of the mind. Math, physics, and chemistry were concrete; they followed rules and logic. She could wrap her mind around them. But people were interesting, too —even if their acts and their choices lacked logic.

"So you like banking, but are not passionate about it?"

"That's fair enough." Her father laughed. "Very perceptive of you."

2003

The lab was dim, its black benches and white cabinets a perpetual contrast. The rest of the benches on her side sat unoccupied this week. It was a glorified warehouse, with its high ceilings and all the space.

Ruth's company, Bay Flavor, could win the prize for the most pretentious name among food research labs. The pun represented by a photorealistic bay leaf on the company logo was an insider joke. In any case, flavors were just one of the many food-related contracts the company received from all over the country. It could be QC, or an investigation of superior components to meet the client's requirements. Or packaging. Whatever it was, it involved tedious work. It included a lot of equipment calibration and tons of record-keeping.

This job was what allowed her to work on her dissertation. Luckily, she had taken Food Chemistry, making her eligible for any number of mindless positions. But she wanted to do research— something meaningful, a long-term project, perhaps in the medical sphere. Most of the better jobs of that type required a PhD. And she had less than two years to finish hers.

A soft knock interrupted Ruth's thoughts. She looked up.

Inspector Rodriguez.

Rodriguez led the investigation of her father's death. His broad face was pleasant and slightly indifferent. A small smile enlivened it, not too merry for the occasion, just polite. His graying hair was all over the place. He wore a simple but well-fitting gray suit. His eyes of the same color were inquisitive, but not threatening.

"Miss Hanson, how are you? Do you mind if I ask you a few questions?"

"Not at all. Have you found out something? Have a seat."

The Inspector pulled over a rolling chair. His large body occupied it to its full extent. He leaned back, looked around. "So, this is work?"

"This is work."

He nodded respectfully. After a pause, he reached into his jacket pocket and retrieved a plastic evidence bag.

"Ma'am, we found this in your father's office."

Something small was inside—some kind of card. He showed the bag to Ruth.

It was a driver's license. She was perplexed, looked closer. "This is my father!"

The inspector's face was neutral. Ruth looked again. Next to the photo was a name, David Conrad. *What the hell?*

"Did you know your father was using a false identity?" Rodriguez's eyes were firm on hers.

"Where did you find that thing?"

"Can you please answer my question?"

"No, of course, I didn't know. How would I know? Where did you find it?"

"In his desk at work. A hidden compartment." Rodriguez sounded apologetic, reluctant to add another layer to Ruth's tragedy.

"What does it mean?"

"We don't know yet. He had his real ID on him when he died. Does this name sound familiar? David Conrad." The inspector's finger pointed toward the plastic bag in his other hand.

"I don't think so. I mean, it sounds like a common name, one of those you've heard thousands of times."

"Do you remember your father mentioning it?"

"No." As she said this, Ruth was uncertain if she could truly account for everything ever mentioned in her presence. "No, I don't think so."

"Well, Miss Hanson, thank you for your time." The inspector rose, storing the plastic bag in his jacket pocket.

"Wait! Don't you have any new information? Why was he in El Cerrito?"

Ruth hadn't expected the conversation to be over so soon. A fake ID was unusual for a Bank of America executive—it was utterly perplexing.

"No, I'm afraid not. But we'll let you know as soon as we discover anything."

"Thank you."

Ruth wondered, for the first time, if her father's death would ever be explained.

CHAPTER FOUR

1983, DRESDEN

Uncle Fritz agreed to cooperate? The Stasi's insinuation is a wedge in Ulrike's head. The small room feels tighter. Her chest is constricted as she struggles to decide how to respond. It seems impossible—but nothing is truly impossible in this place. Doctor Vogel's eyes are tight on Ulrike, observing her reaction. Lenin's steely stare from the poster is trained on her, confident and vicious. *Help them? How am I supposed to help?* Her chair is stiff under her, uncomfortable on purpose.

None of this is fair. What am I supposed to say?

"I'm not a liar."

Joyful screams of kids playing outside are sinister in this setting. Perhaps a recording, not the real thing?

"We're interested in your parents. We've been monitoring them for some time. You know what they are involved in." A statement, not a question.

Mama and Papa? What did they do now? Again, Ulrike wishes

24

they were here. She must track what she says—but she's exhausted, barely able to collect her thoughts.

"We don't really need your testimony. This is just an opportunity, you see. We're trying to be humane and give you a chance to come clean with us and help yourself. Your country has done everything for you. You have free medical care, free education. Now it's your turn to do something for your country." Vogel is calm, his every pore exuding blame, bewilderment at the extent of Ulrike's moral failure. His empty eyes remain on hers, barely blinking. *He's an owl focused on its prey.* His left eyebrow twitches.

"What can I do?" Ulrike asks to break the staring contest.

"Telling us about your parents' activities would be a good start." A small smirk flashes on the Stasi's face.

"What activities?" To keep her hands from shaking, Ulrike keeps them in her lap, folded, holding one another tightly.

"Your parents must have discussed their plans. They must have said things. Things critical of the socialist way of life, of our leaders. Do they listen to Western radio?" He pauses a moment, his nasty eyes eating away at her face. "They do, they do, I can see it in your eyes." His teeth glint in a fake smile.

They do, now and then. Everyone does.

"No, they don't."

The man's face relaxes into a contemptuous grin. "Very well then. We'll just note that you didn't want to cooperate."

"I'm cooperating! Am I supposed to make things up?"

"You haven't given me anything yet. You must give me something, Schumacher. Give me something."

What am I supposed to give him? Maybe Vogel is not as certain about his case as he pretends to be. He becomes distracted, shuffles the paperwork in the folder. From her position, Ulrike can see that some of the documents feature her family's pictures.

Think fast. Think fast. "What are my parents accused of, exactly?"

All of her shakes a little, but she hopes the interrogator won't notice. *He probably noticed before I did.*

Vogel sighs. He takes a pack of Marlboros out of his shirt pocket, lights up with a fancy silver-looking lighter. The man's moves are practiced, deliberate, as if he were performing the act of smoking. This must be how the Stasi exist: performing, not living. This is how the entire country of GDR operates.

"They are accused of anti-government work." Vogel's face is sincere, almost conspiratorial—as if he were sharing secret case details they both should be excited about. "The two of them help traitors escape into the FRG." He winks as if this notion were most hilarious. "They have a system. We know all about it, but it will help *you* to separate yourself from your parents' activities. You're just a kid. From what I understand, you're hoping to take your A levels. You tell us all you know, and we'll see what we can do so your life is uninterrupted." He loses concentration, shuffles through the paperwork again, finds something, and stares at it for a few seconds, nodding with a satisfied expression. "Now, tell me what your parents were planning."

"They've never talked about it in front of me."

The moment she says it, she's afraid. Her phrasing suggested there is an "it," that they talk about "it" when she's not around. Ridiculous. *From now on, shorter sentences.*

The interrogator smiles and nods a few times. "Surely they must have said something that sounded unusual at one time or another."

Ulrike is silent. *Unusual? What's usual?*

"Okay, okay, let's take a break." The Stasi remains cheerful. "Would you like a sandwich? I'll have my secretary make you one."

Is there a secretary? Is anything real in this place? Will the sandwich be poisoned?

2002, BERKELEY

The gently rattling BART train propels Ulrike along, her brain scattered, jumping from a client's website project to Peter to her lover, Dietrich. The train is semi-occupied at this midday hour. A little girl across from Ulrike keeps staring, her face inscrutable as in a poker game.

It's a short walk from Downtown Berkeley station. Straight on Allston past the empty Martin Luther King Jr. Park. *Nice fucking suburban houses, a million dollars each.* A left on Grant. The small white cottage hides behind the main house. Ulrike opens her purse and digs out the key from its own little pocket. *These days, every small thing gets a special container. As if being near another item or another person has become a liability. And sometimes it is—who the hell am I to deny that?*

She unlocks the door. The house is dark and silent. *Dietrich's not here yet, asshole. Late as usual.*

Dietrich's lateness may be intentional, marking territory—just to show her that he is not the one who wants this most. Neither is she. The first few months were exciting, as they tend to be. Now, the differences between Peter and Dietrich have evened out. The two men are surprisingly similar.

Her cigarette has reached the end of burning, a dead bud between her fingers.

Heading home is the logical thing to do, but Ulrike resents that as she resents all things predictable. She has been trained to oppose any form of control. She thinks of Honecker, the GDR leader whose miniature head, embedded deeply in her brain, keeps spouting nonsense, reminding her to doubt everything.

She tucks the cigarette butt under the orange pot, home to a small cactus that looks content, unlikely to be displeased. Dietrich hates finding these smelly artifacts, but Ulrike enjoys teasing him. Humor may be the one thing that keeps this affair going.

The ridiculous delay reminds her of those evenings at Uncle Franz's in the late seventies, waiting for her father to pick her up. Ulrike was eight or nine. An invalid, Uncle Franz was on a government pension, his paralysis caused by something from World War II he preferred not to discuss. His was *the silent generation.*

He rode around the apartment in a bright-red imported wheelchair, quiet like death, with a small, forced smile on his well-trimmed face. He was a solitary person—and putting it this way is the understatement of the century. Ulrike could tell her presence bothered him like hell on steroids—the fact of another human being's existence in his vicinity. He would leave Ulrike in the kitchen with her books and work in his room, presumably on some of his weird research he preferred not to discuss.

Usually her father was due by seven but didn't make it. As the time approached, the premonition of relief invaded her uncle's demeanor anytime he emerged from his inner sanctum. He became more relaxed, even extending an occasional genuine smile and an offer of tea. But when seven came and passed, tension began to mount. *What was all that about, really? Was he a drug addict awaiting his shot the moment Dad picked me up? A gay man hiding like other gay men did in that stupid former country?*

Uncle Franz may be dead by now. He is or was her mother's older brother. The Stasi succeeded in breaking at least that connection in their family.

She was twenty-four when her parents crossed the ocean to join her. Emigration was a rebirth for them—not only a chance to live in a free society, but a second shot at their marriage. To be sure, they did a laughable job of it, splitting up three years later.

The front door swings open, interrupting her thoughts. Dietrich always arrives with abundant energy.

"Hey, baby!" His voice fills the small cottage. He is an average-looking guy with a regular build. Some muscle but nothing special. A pleasant face, but not beautiful. *Is this all I deserve in this fucking world of billions of men?* He is intelligent but not particularly interesting.

Dietrich squeezes her in one of his powerful embraces. Ulrike is small, lost in all that male power. His smell, his touch penetrate her defenses. They kiss passionately, their hands exploring each other's bodies. After a week apart, fucking is the first order of business. One quality she likes in Dietrich, a thing of no minor importance: he is good at oral sex. Peter, non-committal on that front, has some part of his Catholic upbringing still lurking in him. He is somewhat uncomfortable with a woman's anatomy.

This thing with Dietrich is not helping my already complicated life. As it is, I barely have time to get my work done. These BART rides to Berkeley, what a crazy thing to do. What is it about Dietrich? Did my fucked up GDR past make me so sick of rules that I must break them all the time? Not exactly fair to Peter. And all the secrecy. I'm supposed to be sick of secrets. I'll have to do something. Something.

CHAPTER FIVE

2003

Ruth stumbled out of bed and flipped her laptop open.

What she wanted and feared jumped at her. A response from Peter Litmanowic.

Morning shadows lay quietly on the floor. Ruth closed her eyes and rubbed them with her palms. The sounds of the busy street penetrated the room. All this was too much.

Without reading the email, Ruth walked over to the semi-drawn blinds and opened them all the way. *A colorless day.* The ocean's massive presence invaded the neighborhood, corrupting its colors and its mood. Water was corrosive, omnipresent. Good old H_2O. And salt, all that salt, our favorite $NaCl$.

Ruth valued this bit of time before work, an opportunity to fully inhabit herself. She thought of her hero, Marie Curie, who had named Polonium after her homeland and then died from exposure. She was the brightest scientist ever and a beautiful woman to boot with her intense, inquisitive eyes. *What would Marie do if she were in my shoes?* Ruth imagined being compared to Marie in some distant, brilliant future where Ruth's scientific contributions merited that. There was much work to do in the meantime.

She stretched, walked over to the kitchen, and fed the toaster. Eight seconds in the microwave, a perfect time to soften the butter without melting it. The timer-activated coffee machine had already sprung into action. The beautiful aroma rendered the air optimistic.

Ruth's black coffee mug was warm in her hand as she carried it back. She used a red mug at work for contrast. The plate with two slices of toast sat neatly on her palm. She brought the coffee to her face, closed her eyes, enjoying the aroma, and took a satisfying sip. Taking a big bite of toast, she sat down in front of her laptop.

Dear Ruth,

Thank you
I don't know what to say
I want to ask you
I don't know what to ask, but I want to ask you about it. I need to know everything there is to know.
Sorry, can't think straight. Can we meet?
Thank you,

Peter

Ruth read the email a second time. She imagined herself in Peter's place. She would have wanted to know more. But immediately, the other side of the coin came to mind. She was supposed to have something meaningful to contribute—but the entire episode had happened so fast it was difficult to describe it in more than a few words.

It didn't make sense that such a monumental thing—the extinguishment of a life—should be so instant as to leave no story to tell.

What she felt may find words only when she was face to face with Peter.

She had no choice, now.

* * *

Ruth had forgotten about her colleague's return.

"Jingfei! Great to see you."

"You too, Ruth. You too."

They hugged. The lab was empty of life, its neat bays excessive and mechanical. The sun, less of a saboteur downtown than in Outer Richmond, streaked in warm lines along the linoleum's light orange.

"How was your vacation?"

"Well..." A semi-incredulous expression appeared on Jingfei's round, well-rendered face. A face that received meticulous care to supplement its intrinsic qualities, making Jingfei ageless. Ruth knew that Jingfei was in her early sixties, but one wouldn't think so by looking at her.

"Well?"

"I met someone." Jingfei's eyes lit with joy.

"Wow! Wonderful! Who is he?"

"You won't believe it, Ruth. He's a businessman. A millionaire."

"A millionaire?" Ruth felt disoriented.

"Yes. He proposed to me." Jingfei sowed her hand, an enormous diamond shining from a golden ring on a long finger.

"That's wonderful," Ruth managed to say, still not quite understanding the situation.

"I know. What are the chances of meeting someone on a ten-day cruise? Maybe this is why people go on cruises."

"How did it happen?" Ruth was surprised, but only partly incredulous, partly delighted for her co-worker. It was a treat to be happy for someone.

"There's this bar on the second deck. It's not usually my thing, but you're on a ship all day, and there's not much to do. On Day Six, I'd already read both books I'd brought with me. I was just sipping my drink and minding my business, getting sad and desperate about the whole trip. Then I notice this guy staring..."

Ruth's attention was fading. It was too early in the day for the extended story, but she didn't want to be rude.

"Anyway, I asked him why, and he says, *you're the most beautiful woman I have ever seen, and just looking at you is more happiness than any man is worth.* Can you imagine that?"

Jingfei paused as if to conjure the most accurate image but instead extended her hand to demonstrate the ring once more. Its gold enhanced with minerals was a mere fusion of chemical elements to Ruth, who'd never mastered a fascination with jewelry.

"I'm sorry, I'm talking too much. I'm so happy." Jingfei looked flustered as if she'd overexposed herself.

"No, no, not at all. I'm so happy for you." Ruth was ready for her coffee.

There seemed to be something fishy about Jingfei's story, but it was not Ruth's responsibility to point that out. Did she have to be friends with Jingfei? So clear-cut, so superficial. *Am I superficial in my own way?* Ruth had never been good at making friends. Her one good friend, Sarah, had moved back to the East Coast after college.

Is there room for friendships in my life?
I don't think so.
I hope so.

1983

"Mom, why are all the girls at school so dumb?" Ruth tried, but failed, to catch her mother's eye.

"What makes you say so, Ruthie?" Linda laughed, which was odd: usually, she laughed only at her own jokes. Too bad. Ruth's question hadn't been a joke.

"They just care about girl stuff, you know." Ruth didn't want to elaborate. Surely Mom would understand.

The May sun shone heavily on Market Street without producing much warmth. Ruth was glad to have her sweater on. They had to pick up Linda's shoes from a repair shop near Montgomery Street.

"Girl stuff?"

"Yes. Dating. Who to marry when the time comes."

"What's wrong with that?" Linda's blue eyes scanned Ruth's face as if checking for surface defects.

"Isn't that kind of life boring?"

As soon as she said that, Ruth felt bad. *Shit, shit, shit.* She was talking to a stay-at-home mom. And here she was, criticizing future moms. The moment felt bitter with the realization of her growing split from her mother. *I'll never allow my life to be constrained in that way. I'll have a career. A career as a chemist.*

"What does it feel like, being a housewife?" She used the old-fashioned term intentionally.

As usual, Linda simply ignored her question.

Ruth had had enough. She stopped in her tracks.

"Mom! Why don't you answer?"

"Come on, come on." Linda looked intensely uncomfortable; she still avoided eye contact. "Don't make a scene. Let's just keep walking."

"I'm not making a scene; you are. I asked you a question, and you ignored it. If you were going to just ignore me, why did you take me along?"

"Okay, okay. What about dumb girls? What about housewives? I've had a lovely life raising you and caring for the family. Your dad didn't seem to mind paying for it. What's wrong with that?"

"Nothing." Ruth was out of energy and out of thoughts for this pointless discussion.

The truth was, not only were the girls in her class boring, but her parents, too, were in that category. Ruth had felt this before—but only now did this conclusion arise in her mind with full clarity. Her parents never talked about books or ideas—stuff that mattered. They discussed trivial things: food, travel, promotions.

Luckily, books were on her side. Since before she'd learned to read, age six, she'd been drawn to them.

"Why don't you come watch TV with us?" her parents would inquire as she sat with her nose stuck in a thick volume.

She couldn't explain her love of books, but she needed more than the TV that repeated itself every day. Even the shows her parents watched were the same from night to night. She wanted to imagine more.

CHAPTER SIX

2002, SAN FRANCISCO

The tall ceilings supported by the unique upside-down Vs are among Ulrike's favorite features at this posh place named Café Claude. The yellow walls, wood floors, and off-red leather seats all contributes to a tasteful, unobtrusive vibe. But Ulrike can't seem to enjoy it just now. *Being broke, needing more work, needing to finish the current project, broke, work, projects, broke. Why are my thoughts always cycled on the same and more of the same, like a ferret on meth?* Peter is going on and on about her art aspirations. She should appreciate his interest in her—yet she can't seem to focus.

"What if we turned that area between the bed and the back wall into a collapsible studio for you?" Peter's face is kind and excited.

"Thanks for the thought, Peter. It might work. But what about all the mess I might make?" She can't sort her unruly bunch of reactions into neat categories. *To hell with categories, anyway.*

"You could cover things up with plastic," Peter says. "We'll figure it out."

For the last few months or few years, Ulrike's felt this urge to lash out, to sting, bite, scratch, bodily or verbally. *It's not me, it's something other than me, inside. Something I must be feeding. Otherwise, the nasty thing would have long dried up like a fig.*

They order two Devil Kisses, their favorite drink.

"I'm sorry." She follows the waiter's back with her eyes instead of making eye contact.

"For what?"

"For not jumping at the mini-studio idea. I know you're trying to help. And I should take you up on it. I really should. I'll buy some plastic. Soon." Ulrike looks around nervously, grasping her hands. "Excuse me." She gets out of her seat. "I'll be right back."

In the bathroom, Ulrike rests her arms on the wash basin and examines her face in the mirror—the same old façade she has scrutinized so many times before. The same blonde hair. The face is rounder than it used to be.

Suddenly, the notion of returning to the table is incomprehensible, an immense pressure added to the already mounting pile. Ulrike picks up her bag and leaves the restroom. In the back of the stylish dining room, Peter's face is turned toward the window, a vague smile still on his lips. Ulrike stops, observing him for a moment or two. *What a beautiful man.* But the outside door is within arm's reach. Without another thought, Ulrike pulls it open and walks out.

The street is intense: a bath of noise, a whirlpool of colors. These American cities with their incredible architectural contrasts, the new and the slightly old. She heads down Kearny, an eccentric street that collapses into a building when it reaches Market. She crosses Sutter, then Post. The city distracts her with its busy splendor and its multifaceted purpose. She reaches Market and turns right, keeps walking southwest, away from the Embarcadero and toward San Francisco's modest hills, their tops peeking amid the buildings.

1983, DRESDEN

The small room is oppressive. Ulrike can't bear another interruption. She longs to be out of here. Vogel picks up the phone, apparently to reach the secretary. *Why would he bother with a sandwich for me?* She observes him in this non-interactive moment.

His gray eyes stare somewhere to her left, his lips pursed a little. He's just had a haircut. His thin face is shrunk into itself, the threat dialed down a notch. His movements are reluctant, abdicating energy. *He doesn't want to be here.*

Seconds crawl, Vogel stuck with a phone to his face. He gives up, swears under his breath. "No one wants to work in this country. No wonder socialism is under attack. The failure starts inside us."

He walks out.

Great—now he will be even more pissed at me because of some stupid secretary and some sandwich. Being alone in that darkened room brings back the tension in her muscles, the pressure of air sucking her in. The white Lenin keeps staring from the ominous poster while Honecker observes from the portrait, his face dignified. Ulrike can't concentrate, her thoughts going over minor events of the day unrelated to this present challenge. *Think, think.* The children's voices outside have disappeared. *What am I supposed to say?* She doesn't have anything to say. *Scheisse!*

Vogel returns with a small tray. Two sandwiches, two cans of Coca Cola instead of the familiar Club Cola bottles, the GDR's dreary alternative. He places the tray on the desk between them, a hand gesture inviting her to partake.

Is this a trick? Am I supposed to reject the Western goods?

Ulrike makes no move.

As if reading her thoughts, the Stasi flips the tab on his own can, causing that unique whiz Ulrike doesn't get to hear often. Despite all the advantages of socialism, East Germany hasn't mastered canned drinks. Vogel takes a gulp.

"Go ahead." He points to the food again. "Everyone needs to eat."

Ulrike has trouble deciding. *What if they are videotaping the whole conversation? They probably are.* Would accepting the food and the Coca Cola be seen in a questionable light by her family and by other critics of the regime? But if she has nothing to say to the Stasi, what's wrong with eating the sandwich? Its smell is a fairy tale. *I would be eating my enemy's food and giving nothing back.*

Something in her resists.

"I'm not hungry." Her stomach rumbles, but the rejection feels good.

"Suit yourself. Won't you even have a drink?"

Act friendly. Ulrike picks up her can, her fingers hesitant as she fiddles with the tab. The design looks flimsy and vulnerable. Still, the ring's thin edge is rough on her fingers. In addition to being scared, she is now self-conscious about her lack of skill in can opening.

The tab comes out with much less difficulty than she expected, nearly causing her to drop the can. A hiss as the jinni is released, the crack, the breaking seal, the whole tab in the middle coming off its hinges. The design screams its cool Western magic. The Coca Cola tastes similar and different from Club Cola, with much of the nasty sweetness removed. The metal is cold in Ulrike's hand. The bubbles nip at her mouth.

Vogel observes her with a smirk. He takes a gulp from his can and a big bite from his sandwich. *Apparently, he was never taught to keep his mouth shut while chewing.* Ulrike's famished; the food commands her attention. Even across the table, she can smell the delicious flavors emanating from Vogel's sandwich.

"Tell me, what are you going to be?" Vogel asks, his face neutral as his jaws do the work.

She must pause a moment. The faces staring down at her—they make her confused. Her chair is increasingly uncomfortable.

"I'd like to be an artist."

Now I'll never be one. My life is over.

"An artist, eh? So you think being an artist is the best thing you can do for socialism? What's wrong with being a worker at the factory? A nurse? An engineer? You could be delivering mail. Your country gives you so many opportunities. Doesn't it?"

"Yes."

There is a pause. Ulrike is tempted to explain that she didn't mean any offense to factory workers, but she stops herself. New to this interrogation business, she already understands and feels viscerally: here, any answer can be wrong.

"Why do you want to be an artist?" Vogel looks grumpy as if he'd expected her to react differently.

"Socialism has a human face. We must show the enemy that we have a stronger and more genuine spiritual and intellectual life than the West. This is what art is for. Socialist art represents factory workers, mail staff, and all other citizens." She's reciting propaganda lines; they both know it. This is expected. She is willing to play along in this way. She is slightly grateful for the Coca Cola and the offer of food.

"Yes, yes," Vogel says absent-mindedly, seemingly having lost any interest in the topic. Another bit of silence follows. Ulrike avoids eye contact with Lenin and Honecker. Instead, she looks down at the desk between her and Vogel.

"When did your parents start smuggling people to the West?"

She swallows, almost chokes, coughs.

"They are not." She coughs again. "I don't know anything about it."

"*Scheisse!* Think, child, think!"

Unbelievable. He expects me to betray my own parents. Do others go through this? Smuggling people to the West—is this why Papa leaves some evenings? His chess club? This could be bad for all of them—and good at the same time, a brave thing.

"I *am* thinking," she says. "There's nothing to think. Nothing comes up. How's it even possible? The border is two hundred kilometers from here, isn't it?"

"Keep your voice down!" Vogel's face is sharp, frightening in a new way. "So my information is wrong, is it?" He sighs and levels her with a contemptuous stare. "You're defending your father after everything he's done to your poor mother?"

Again, a small silence hangs. But then, Ulrike can't help asking, "What did he do?"

"I shouldn't be the one to tell you, but what the hell, you made me. I mean all his love affairs."

"What love affairs?" Ulrike is shocked by this theme, incongruously mixed in with smuggling foreigners, with this small room. *What the hell kind of world am I in?*

"Oh, well. We better not talk about it. Here is my number." He hands Ulrike a small paper rectangle with numbers scribbled on it. "Take it and call me soon. Don't talk to your parents about this. If you do, they'll reveal it to the people they're working with. We'll know too. We always know. As for you, you'll be in way more trouble than you already are. There's a better choice. Help me a little, and we'll see what we can do for you and your family." Vogel consults his watch. "Don't answer now, think about it first."

Ulrike's hand shakes with the piece of paper in it. For a few seconds, she stares at Vogel in fear and disgust.

"Can I go?"

"I'll give you a ride back."

She sets her half-empty can on the desk and stands. "I'll walk. It's not far."

"Suit yourself." Vogel's smile is contemptuous, as if Ulrike is too predictable in refusing the ride. "I'll walk you out."

On the stairs, Ulrike avoids looking at Vogel. What if he changes his mind about letting her go? They run into a young woman with a baby, apparently headed to one of the floors above.

The Stasi are just some of the residents in this building, as in every other in the GDR.

"Remember," Vogel barks behind her. "Either you tell us something, or your parents tell us something about you. Your uncle has already given us plenty. Soon we'll know the rest. I assure you that waiting until that happens is the worst-case scenario for your entire family. Cooperate, and we will go easy on you. Think carefully and do the right thing."

Ulrike nods without looking back. Then she is out of the building, the air outside like balm. She breathes. She has escaped this time, but she knows her escape is temporary and will always be from now on.

CHAPTER SEVEN

2003

On her way home from the lab, the bus was crowded. A few feet from Ruth, an old woman clutched her brown purse tightly to her chest as if afraid of being robbed. Fatigue imbued her posture, her body nearly hanging off the rail she held with her free hand. Her eyes stared into a sad nowhere above Ruth's shoulder. A high school kid in the seat facing the old lady didn't even raise his eyes. His ears were snuffed out with miniature headphones.

Ruth felt depressed. With this came doubts about Jingfei's story. And what about Ulrike? Ulrike had no more doubts. Thinking of Ulrike made Ruth feel guilty about her discontent.

When she got home, she opened her laptop and quickly typed,

Dear Peter,

Most evenings work for me after 6pm or so. Saint Frank Coffee on Polk is not far from my parents' house. I like it,

but any place you choose would be equally good. I'm so
sorry about what happened, and if I can help in any way.

She deleted the last bit. How could she possibly help?

She pressed *Send*.

* * *

Ruth scanned Saint Frank's elegant setting. Peter Litmanowic was
already there. He looked the same as on his profile picture, but he
wasn't smiling. Ruth walked up to the table and shook his hand.
His face was heavy with grief. He wore jeans and a simple green T-
Shirt with a washed-out slogan. Ruth was dressed almost identi-
cally, apart from her shoes.

"I'm sorry," she said. "I don't know if this was a good idea. I
hope so." She'd prepared this remark, knowing the beginning of this
conversation might be difficult.

"No...yes...why not. Please sit down. I'm Peter." He paused.
"Obviously, you know that."

Peter was awkward but didn't seem embarrassed about it. Ruth
had prepared other things to say, but none of them came to mind
now. She wished for a cappuccino to busy herself with; she should
have ordered first. Now it would be awkward to interrupt the
conversation.

I can't face this without caffeine. It could be my last chance.

"I'm sorry. Do you mind if I get a drink?" she blurted out.

"No, no. Of course not. Please go ahead."

Ruth walked up to the counter, feeling terrible about doing this
instead of giving her full attention to Peter. Saint Frank's wood
paneling, the simple and honest balance of white and brown, the
elongated shape—these attributes had always calmed her. She'd
grown used to the place. A good-looking barista with a diverse
collection of rings in his nose greeted her cheerfully. She ordered.

"I'll bring it over when it's ready." The barista's gigantic smile was an odd contrast to the mood of her meeting with Peter. "Don't you worry, honey."

It was too late to buy time; she had to face Peter's grief. This is why she was here in the first place. Her legs and torso hovered in a wobbly universe where the laws of physics hesitated. Ruth forced herself to walk back and landed in her chair opposite Peter.

"Thanks for reaching out." Peter was so good-looking he made her feel awkward. *It's most inappropriate of me to think of his looks, now.*

"I thought it was my responsibility." She hesitated, searching for the right words. "I don't know why. Somehow it made sense. Did it? I don't know." She was surprised anew at the lack of verifiable reasons for this meeting.

"You said she just veered into another lane." His eyes stared intensely into hers. "Why? Could you see her? I mean, could you see *her* inside the car?"

Ruth closed her eyes, remembering.

"No, no. There was a glare." The highway, the cars, and the ocean came alive in her mind, retrieved by the brain's helpful chemistry. "She kept going straight where the lane curved as if she hadn't noticed the curve. She must have gotten distracted. It didn't take long. Let me think."

Almost two weeks had passed. Ruth went over the memory as she had done many times. The white car's direction and velocity, the estimated weight of the tomato truck.

"It took just three seconds, maybe four."

"They tell me...they tell me that...she didn't suffer. Do you think that's true?"

The barista arrived with Ruth's cappuccino, placing it carefully on the table. An awkward interruption, but it felt good to be distracted, to set the accident aside for a moment. The barista moved flamboyantly through space; Ruth noticed his long fake eyelashes. She appreciated her city where people could be themselves.

"Can I get you beautiful people something else?"

"No, thanks," Ruth said.

"Not for the moment." A smile flashed on Peter's exhausted face. Something about how easily he accepted that *beautiful people* bit appealed to Ruth.

"Sorry." For no reason, she tracked the retreating barista with her eyes. "No. No, I don't think she suffered. There wasn't enough time."

"I see. That's good. That's what they told me." Peter's expression was tense, inward.

She kept pushing her mind to remember slower than the real event, in more detail. The dread of the inevitable collision preceding the accident itself, a death that had already established itself in the eye of the observer but not the subject.

"An awful thing," she offered, something warm and meaningless.

"Yes, an awful thing." Peter nodded several times. "Tell me again what you saw."

"The white car...Ulrike's car...it was going straight, you know. What I mean is, the highway curved, but she must not have noticed."

Ruth was repeating herself, fighting back tears. Frustratingly, there was little more to say. The event was sufficiently described with the simplest words. But Peter was listening, and Ruth felt obligated to keep talking as if more were required to honor Ulrike's death properly.

"The car was just going straight. It was subtle. It was a slight curve. It really was as tragic and simple as this. If it were another car, maybe it would have made a difference. But she hit a truck, a huge truck. You already know this. I'm sure I haven't told you anything new. But the real reason I wanted to talk to you is that I was there. I was affected. Yes, affected—that's the word."

Ruth paused. Sometimes words came out surprising to herself, as in chemistry.

"In some way, I've become a different person. Maybe that matters? I keep wondering what may have distracted her. Who knows? She may have been looking for something, or trying to tackle something: an address, a coffee cup. She probably took her eyes off the road for too long, that's all. I'm so, so sorry."

Ruth was crying. She was embarrassed to do so in this posh cafe, in front of this poor man who had more reason to cry. Through her tears, she could see the barista observe them with a tactful expression. Peter's face was distracted but concerned as if he was doing his best to be here in the moment with her.

She pulled herself together and blew her nose with a paper napkin that had a few touches of coffee on it. "I'm sorry. It's been a difficult month."

"Yes," Peter responded absent-mindedly. His brown eyes returned to her. "Thank you, Ruth. Thank you. This makes me feel better. *Feel better?* Is that the right way to say it?" He disappeared into his question for a second or two. "Sharing it with someone is helpful. Someone who was there."

"How long were you married?"

Peter's face was intense and reflective as he stared somewhere over Ruth's right shoulder. Seconds passed.

"Six years." His face stilled as if he were trying to evaluate the significance of such a period.

Immediately, Ruth felt at odds. Had her question been too personal?

"Six years..." she repeated, avoiding the responsibility for the next thing to say.

Peter sipped something that may have been green tea. Ruth

took a sip of her cappuccino. It was excellently crafted and conceived, happy molecules making their way to her brain and already waking it up through the mere anticipation of their arrival. *Bless old Pierre Jean Robiquet, the father of caffeine.* The helpful cow protein softened the bitterness. Ruth followed up with another large sip. Still, Peter sat there, thinking, staring into space.

Ruth chose to break the extended pause. "Tell me about Ulrike."

Peter looked straight at her. "Tell me about you first, if you don't mind. I'm sorry I haven't asked earlier. What do *you* do?"

"I'm a chemist."

"A chemist? Nice. I've met a few chemists at the office. Interesting people. Where do you work?"

"A small food chemistry lab." Ruth was embarrassed to tell. "I'm only there until I finish my PhD. I hope to have a lab of my own in ten years or so."

It felt good to announce her ambitions, even if she knew that the pleasure originated in her own insecurity. Her whole statement had a tacky show-off quality. *Who in the world claims her plans as credit? Only desperate people, like myself.*

"That's exciting. Very exciting." Peter's watering eyes were seeing something else.

"Tell me about Ulrike," she repeated, anxious to reframe the conversation.

"Okay." Again, Peter nodded a few times. "I'll try." He closed his eyes for a moment. "She was smart, talented, beautiful. She had a perfect eye for visual balance. She was a web designer. She used to be an artist." Peter paused.

How many images of Ulrike had passed through his mind? Those helpful neurons, wonders of chemistry.

"She was from East Germany." Peter regarded her inquisitively. "The GDR, you know?"

"Yes, yes, of course. When did she move here?"

Ruth remembered her naïve high school essay about the countries of the communist bloc. East Germany. How strange that the theme should resurface in her life.

"1991. Soon after the Reunification. She was twenty-two at the time. She was from Dresden." Peter trailed off, apparently flooded by memories. His face was lost, sunk into itself. A beautiful face.

"What was she like?"

Peter made eye contact again. His eyes were firm but kind.

"Ulrike? She was exuberant. She was sad. She was full of ideas. Sometimes she could be a little crabby. Her life wasn't easy, you know." Peter was getting animated, his face inspired. "She kept trying to catch up. She grew up in a fake, ideological world. As an artist, she had no chance with the kind of work she wanted to do, back there. When she moved to the States, she got a degree in German History but couldn't get a job."

Ruth had lived with her latest boyfriend, Vladko, for over a year, yet she barely knew him and could never describe him as eloquently.

"She took classes to be a web designer," Peter continued. "It was a good time, the mid -90s. Things were going well for her. Then the dot com crash hit, and it became harder to find work." Peter paused and scratched his chin, darkened by several days of stubble. "She was complicated, you know. People are complicated. I'm probably every bit as difficult. She wasn't the best at dealing with these challenges. Clients. Especially here, in a new culture."

Every few statements, Peter took a sip from his cup as if his throat needed frequent irrigation. Perhaps he still suffered the injustices in Ulrike's life that she herself no longer faced. *No one would be as affected by my death.*

"She was reserved. Sometimes I wondered if she loved me." A puzzled expression showed up on Peter's face. "Other times, I knew she did."

"Were you happy?" Ruth instantly regretted asking another difficult question.

"Yes." Peter was unhesitant. "We had our issues, our fights, like everyone. But we were happy. I know I was. And she...she was sad sometimes, but she was also happy. I think she was, anyway. With some people, you can't always tell."

"True." Ruth remembered Vladko's gloomy days when nothing brought a smile to his face.

Again, Peter disappeared in his thoughts.

This feels so odd. Am I right to be in this man's tragedy? Should I just leave without bothering him further? Facing this person so closely connected to another human being whose death I witnessed feels surreal.

But it was happening, and none of it defied the laws of nature. None of it made any sense either: her father's fake ID, El Cerrito, her mother's nonchalant attitude. The world didn't make sense once you stepped outside the lab. The purity of chemistry didn't survive the pollution of reality.

"How are you doing?" Ruth asked when the silence became too heavy.

Peter thought a while. "I'm surviving. I've gone to work. What else can I say?" These words came out forcefully. "Sorry, I don't mean to be unpleasant. I'm okay. I'm not okay. I'll be okay, but for now, it's down to getting through each day. I keep thinking that I will see her again, any moment. At home, or just in the street somewhere. She might be just around the corner. She always feels just around the corner." He was silent for a while, his face shut down. "This whole thing seems like a horrible mistake. As if someone else was in that car. Maybe even myself."

"Yes. It's unthinkable that it was her."

Immediately, Ruth realized that in saying so, she had claimed a special intimacy with Ulrike she was not entitled to. Was this kind of intimacy desirable, valuable, moral? It didn't feel like a choice. Ulrike's accident had made her a meaningful figure in Ruth's life, even if they'd never met. And now, Ulrike had grown one more layer. It wasn't only her death, but this—the way this sad, elegant man had described her.

CHAPTER EIGHT

As she walks home down the beautiful dusky streets of Dresden, Ulrike debates how to describe the Vogel encounter to her parents. She will not conceal any of it as the Stasi insisted. This would be ridiculous, siding with him instead of her own family. So much of his game was bluff; it had to be.

As she gets close, her heart rate increases. Fear and confusion hang inside her, a red wave. *What if the Stasi arrest them all and turn their place into another of their offices? The Stasi want more Stasi until everyone in the country is one.* She walks up the two flights of stairs. The stairway is clean and simplistic, painted green up to half the wall and yellow from there. As a child, she used to slide her hand along the dividing line. She remembers distinctly having to lift her arm to reach it—and now it's below shoulder level.

"Uli! Where were you?" Her mother is at the kitchen table, correcting students' papers. Inside, the walls are white. The small table is covered with a worn blue vinyl cloth.

"I..."

"Yes?"

"The Stasi. A Stasi picked me up at school. He took me to his office."

"*Scheisse.* Why? What did he want with you?" Her mother jumps up, rushes to her—then acts as if she doesn't know whether to hug her daughter or not. She ends up patting Ulrike on the shoulder in a disconcerting way. Difficulties always make Barbara hesitant and helpless—she is a fun, caring mother when things are good but freezes under duress.

Each moment takes forever. *Mama's face—does it look worried in a normal way, or does it confirm the Stasi's accusation?* Even as she asks herself this, Ulrike feels guilty. Her father might be an enemy of the state. A resister. *This would be a noble role. Would it?* It's all mixed up, tied up in a nasty knot in her head.

"They said...he said that you...that dad is involved in smuggling people to the West."

"Smuggling people to the West?" Her mother laughs bitterly. "Why?"

"Why what, *Mutter?*"

Barbara doesn't respond.

Ulrike has trouble remembering the sequence of her interrogation. She remembers the feeling of being caught, her life being over before it began. *I'll never go to college. I'll never be an artist.*

"He...he said they know all about it. Uncle Franz is cooperating."

"Franz? Franz?" Her mother thinks for a second. "No, dear, no way. The Stasi must have been bluffing." She doesn't sound convinced. "Poor thing, I'm sorry you had to go through it." Barbara stares somewhere to the right of Ulrike. "Let's not do anything until your dad is back from work. You understand, don't you? It must be some mistake. You know how it is. People denouncing one another. Oh, to hell with that. You must be hungry. I'll make something for you."

"Thanks, Mother. He offered me a sandwich, but I refused to eat it."

"A sandwich?" Barbara's face goes blank as if the concept eluded her.

"And a Coca-Cola."

"I see. He was trying to soften you up. Make you trust him. Show you that the State is this big friendly thing you don't need to be afraid of. Good for you for turning it down."

She didn't turn down the Coca-Cola, but it's not that important, or at least she hopes it's not. Vogel's other statement still gnaws at her. It's impossible to leave it out.

"He said dad was having love affairs." Ulrike just throws it out like this without attempting to soften it. She can't keep eye contact. Her heart is beating, and she is almost nauseated from stress.

"Love affairs?" Her mother looks at her, pensive for a moment. "Hmm...Don't believe it, darling. These people always lie." Barbara's stare returns to that other world, her face an expression of martyrdom and perpetual sadness. This isn't Ulrike's favorite in her mother's arsenal of faces. She gives up trying to read what hides behind it.

Barbara stands by the window, facing a bright summer evening. Ulrike sits at the kitchen table. Her hands find the tablecloth's blue vinyl where it almost reaches her knees. A spicy and delicious smell lingers in the air from whatever her mother has cooked. Simple, unthreatened life is over; her mother knows it too. Their country is no longer on their side, which means theirs is no side at all. *Mama will not get a promotion at school. Papa...who even knows what will happen to him. From now on, our lives are unpredictable.*

2002, SAN FRANCISCO

It took three hours and two buses to get home. Ulrike is tired from her exertion, but her mental distress is subdued. She drops her purse on the kitchen counter, pours some water into a glass, and gulps down half of it.

Peter enters the kitchen. "What happened?"

"I'm sorry, Peter," Ulrike says. "It was unfair of me. I felt overwhelmed."

Peter stares incredulously. "So this is all you're going to say? You were overwhelmed. This is why I was stuck waiting for you at the table for twenty minutes, and then had to sneak into the ladies' room, only to find that you weren't there? All sorts of things went through my mind, you know."

Ulrike pauses for a second before answering, her thoughts a wasp's nest. It's tempting to write all reason off, to scream, to deny any responsibility, to say *fuck it* to everything. She is off-balance: depressed, a half-child from a country that no longer exists—the immigrant, the misfit. Then it comes back to her: she is not forced to be a misfit. Other options exist. She doesn't scream. Instead, she says, very calmly,

"I'm sorry. You're right. I don't know how to explain it—it surprised the shit out of me too. I may need to increase my meds. I'll talk to Sally about it."

Peter nods.

"Sorry, I didn't mean to lose my temper." He is embarrassed, his face scrunched in a grimace of regret.

Peter. Oh, Peter. Eloquent, interesting, successful. Tall and good-looking, sexy as it gets. What's wrong with me? She walks up to Peter and slides into an embrace, her body small in his muscular frame.

* * *

"What do you think this gesture meant?" Sally asks.

Ulrike half-reclines on a bright red couch. Sally likes bright colors, one of the many reasons Ulrike has been coming to this room for therapy for the last four years, spending hours and hours and thousands of dollars discussing her pitiful life. Sally leans forward attentively in her blue therapist chair, her hands folded on her lap. She is wearing one of her cool angular outfits, this one in varying shades of purple, and a matching pair of sandals. Sally's taste is all her own. The walls are orange. The space is comfortable and inviting, the way a small art gallery might be.

"Gesture?" Ulrike returns absent-mindedly.

"Walking away from your lunch date with Peter."

"It wasn't a gesture. Just something I had to do. I didn't feel I could stay in that fucking place another minute."

Ulrike hasn't told Sally about Dietrich, a small withholding that feels necessary. She knows Sally will be appalled and would proffer all kinds of good advice on honesty and changing her life, giving up something, making something of the rest. And she would be right.

It would be intolerable.

Brigita is the only one who knows about Dietrich—Brigita, the faraway friend.

"What about that restaurant made you feel this way?" Sally shifts, as if a new question called for a new posture.

Ulrike goes over the memory of Café Claude, its bright abundance, the privileged clientele, the entire history of privilege that has gone into establishments like that. How ironic that she usually enjoys it.

She hates herself when she can't make sense of her own thoughts, as if their texture refused to be linear, as if each thought gave birth to a series of sub-thoughts, originating an unfathomable garden of mental trees.

"It wasn't the place itself. It's Peter. The way he's always so full of good ideas. As if all dreams must come true. As if unfulfilled hopes didn't contribute to our lives. I don't know if I'm clear."

"I'm interested in what you said. *As if unfulfilled hopes didn't contribute to our lives.* Would you care to elaborate?"

"Well." Ulrike pauses. "What we have achieved defines us, but what we strived to achieve defines us too. Our true selves hover somewhere between the two categories."

"I see what you mean." Sally nods. "So Peter pressures you into getting things done in a way that rubs you wrong?"

"Not really. He doesn't pressure me per se." It's difficult to explain as if the world is a fucked up crossword and the words don't fit the way they're supposed to. "It's that he makes it all feel so easy, a practical matter: you just decide, get some plastic, use the room or not use the room. A world full of solutions. And I'm still trying to decide if I even consider myself an artist, you know. Maybe the best thing I could do is forget about painting. Why spend my life trying to do something I'm not equipped to do? An artist's life can be a frustrating one—it's guaranteed to be, and I don't have a fucking clue if I'm the right person for it."

"Have you tried to explain this to Peter?"

The hefty tree outside the window nods its head, egging her on.

"Not like that, no."

"Why not give it a try? He may be more receptive than you expect."

The very thought of trying tires Ulrike out, like dragging a boulder across a dusty city square. A fat crow perches on a branch outside, sending the branch into a minor vibration, its penetrating cry a warning to everyone. Ulrike is tempted to dump the whole dirty Dietrich story after all. Maybe what's really needed is an adult figure who can validate or contest her experience.

"Well, this is a good spot to end on." Sally points at the clock.

CHAPTER NINE

1984

From her bedroom, Ruth could hear her parents in the living room downstairs. The beautiful but aging house on Russian Hill boasted little soundproofing. Ruth was trying to read.

"All these business trips," Mom's voice said. "Why do you have to travel all the time? You know how hard it is to take care of that child alone."

Ruth smirked, unsurprised. Apparently, she wasn't the only one curious about the trips. Her mother's complaint about her meant nothing after so many times—just a dull edge of offense at her mother for not willing to be fair. Lights from the street danced about on the wall opposite Ruth: the steady luminescence of a nearby streetlight, the occasional searching arcs of car lights.

"Linda, darling, you know why." Dad's voice was tense. "Do we have to have this conversation? Besides, Ruthie is just fine. There's nothing difficult about her."

Thanks, Dad! Ruth would love to tune out the voices, but they traveled too easily into her room. She couldn't focus on anything else. Anxiety seeped through the floor right into Ruth's chest, making her restless and uncomfortable in any position.

"Every time you travel, you're never in your room at the right time," Linda's voice raged. "It's like you're unreachable. And when I manage to get through, you never sound as if you're where you say you are."

"Now that's absurd. What do you mean? Not where, for god's sake?"

"Like it's all a bluff. If you're having an affair, just be a man about it and tell me."

Ruth grimaced in her bed.

"I'm not having an affair, darling. I'm not." The voice sounded softer.

Ruth imagined her father looking sincere and concerned, trying to ease the tension. He might have brought out his charming smile. Was the thing about an affair true? It seemed unlikely, but she couldn't explain why. She didn't know what to think of all this.

Ruth refocused on her book, *1984* by George Orwell, their English teacher's nod to the calendar. "When you read, think about the lives people live in the communist countries, even now. Lives without a choice, without human rights. We'll have an essay assignment on this."

Many people in the world had no hand in selecting their leaders and enjoyed no rights to speak of. She'd known all this from the news—but she tried to imagine, really imagine being completely choiceless. Only one party on the ballot, one candidate. And the food. She'd read that in places like Russia or North Korea, one could barely buy food anymore.

What about life at home? Here in San Francisco, it was difficult to miss destitute people living in the street. Her parents explained that these folks were Reagan's nasty heritage. However weird and absent from themselves Mom and Dad might be, they were Democrats, sincere about equality. In a city so diverse, this was essential.

She thought with sadness of some of the girls in her class that came from money. *What do they think about the city that sweats money, but can't take care of a few thousand homeless?*

"Bullshit," her mother screamed downstairs. "I don't believe you!"

Don't they realize I can hear the whole thing?

2003

The city was comprised of predictable pedestrian and traffic patterns. Fulton Street did a reliable job of running along toward the ocean. Peter's sad face was on Ruth's mind. An interesting, distinct face. Ruth was pained by what he was going through. She wanted to help him, but the impossibility of help was obvious. People were not chemistry, where a specific combination of elements produced a predictable result.

People were driven by chemistry, a multifaceted kind, one scientists were still trying to understand. Unpredictable functionality: intuition, chance over logic. The most fascinating thing happened when the borders between the sciences broke down and the disciplines became one another. Life itself was a result of a non-deterministic chemical reaction. Somehow, those early molecules became cells, became alive. How inspiring. If the molecules could do that, everything seemed possible.

Two nuns in need of exercise walked by as Ruth got off the bus. A car honked, another responded. Ruth imagined a third note in the sequence, but it didn't arrive. A teenager stumbled into her, his hand on an oversized coffee cup. The young man mumbled something in apology. Ruth smiled. *At least he appreciates coffee early in his life.*

A warm evening rested lightly upon the city. The beautiful hills, with their architectural growths, guarded her. So much nature in this corner of the world, one always felt safe. Golden Gate Park on her left was real no matter what humans decided to do. The old windmill knew its business of being out of service for years. It rested in its inspirational role. Two blocks ahead, the ocean waited.

A vague alert came up in Ruth's mind: she was forgetting something. Something she was supposed to do. Too much had happened too quickly. She was lost in her life. A few weeks ago, she'd been clear about her reality and her goals. Now, everything was mixed up, too much death mixed in. She couldn't focus on her dissertation. Grief was chemical, an objective factor.

A blue Honda passed, driving down Fulton much slower than the speed limit. Ruth had seen it before. She walked the half-block to her building. The mail lay where it had fallen inside the gate. The key to the inner door was already in her hand—she couldn't remember the moment she'd taken it out.

Strips of shadow from the outside gate cut into the sun's imprint on the ground. For a second, Ruth was disoriented, as if her life itself had been sliced into sections. She recovered her balance and entered. The apartment was chilly, unwelcoming. She dropped everything on the desk and turned on the heat. The sky behind the window was a fragile blue. Any moment, fog might enclose the neighborhood. Water's games. Ruth couldn't help but respect this simple three-atom structure that had managed to make itself the cornerstone of life.

Thinking this made Ruth thirsty, and she walked into the kitchen and poured a glass. She drank the water in three gulps, poured another glass, and drank slowly. *Odd, how the body forgets what it needs, then remembers.*

Ruth walked over to the desk. Her habit was to get through the mail at once, putting aside only the items that required special attention. Clutter and procrastination were her two worst enemies. She had to be organized to succeed.

An electric bill, a promo postcard insisting that Ruth avail herself of a luxury vacation in Mexico. More than 50% of the photo was taken up by another excellent example of that effective molecule, an ocean so evenly blue it might as well have been photoshopped.

A large yellow envelope had no return address. Ruth tore it open.

Dear Miss Hanson,

We are saddened by your father's death. He was a good friend. Please accept our most sincere condolences.

You father had a complicated life, and he may have left something behind that is private and is not to be seen by others. Our request for you is simple. If you find any files or documents, leave them alone. Don't open or read them. Don't tell the authorities. Don't tell anyone. Destroy them.

This may sound mysterious, but it's not. It's simply a matter of business and your father's commitment. Please don't tell your mother about this communication. There are good reasons for this secrecy, and we assure you that trouble for all involved will ensue should you fail to meet our request.

Your father's accident was most unfortunate. Those of us who remain must tidy up after him. Please help us with that. We will not contact you again unless you fail to follow our instructions. We will keep an eye on you to ensure your cooperation. If you go to the police, they will not be able to trace us. We can easily trace you. Our people in the police department will keep us apprised of any moves on your part. Please be reasonable out of respect for your father and his contributions.

Please think of us as your friends, and thank you for your understanding.

The letter was unsigned. Ruth had been holding her breath while she read. Now the need for oxygen manifested itself. She took in a gulp of air. *Is this from some movie, a stupid joke?*

Her first impulse was to call Rodriguez. She went over to the phone, picked it up. Then doubt stepped in. *Our people in the police department.* Ruth thought of her mother, the pointless, spoiled creature she was. *Would calling the cops put Mom in trouble?*

Ruth reread the letter. *Documents? Why would I be the one to find them? I don't even live in the house anymore.*

Her father had lived a secret life. She'd suspected for years, without seeing it clearly. The traces of that shadow life had been present throughout her childhood. And now, a fake ID—and this threat. *Dad, Dad, what kind of mess have you left us in?*

He must have been pursuing noble goals. How am I supposed to sort it out now?

A memory came back. Ruth was six or seven. The two of them were running errands. A lady came up to her dad and sat next to him on the bench in Sue Bierman Park while Ruth enjoyed the playground. The skyscrapers towered over her like grownups over children, admiring themselves for being lost in the sky. The woman wore a dark gray suit.

"Who was the lady?" Ruth asked.

"Someone from work." Her father's expression was neutral, unconcerned.

"What does she do at work?"

Her father thought for a second. His face remained neutral.

"She's a secretary."

Ruth never saw the lady again.

What were Ulrike's parents like? Her childhood? No matter what transpired in my family, she must have had it much worse. Ruth's heart shrank. *I'll never get a chance to ask her.*

1986

Ruth's last class was cancelled. A sunny spring day hung over San Francisco, pulling a light breeze from the Bay. The air was packed with smells. Ruth enjoyed living in a city by the water, among the many other advantages. She passed by Lombard Street Reservoir and the tennis court. A couple of middle-aged ladies in better shape than Ruth hit rapid balls at each other. They waved their colorful futuristic rackets like magic wands.

At seventeen, Ruth felt fully adult, yet she had little control over her life and no alternative to living with her parents, whose fights were as consistent as their avoidance of real conversation.

It was the end of her junior year. She couldn't wait for college: she'd be out from under her parents' gloomy nothing. When Marie Curie wanted to go, most colleges in Poland accepted only male students. Luckily, Ruth was spared that nonsense. She was debating whether to bet on Berkeley or Caltech or to apply to any number of good schools on the East Coast. Caltech was an attractive choice if she could get in—but she much preferred to stay in the Bay Area. Berkeley was among the best; and no place else, anywhere, was as interesting or as liberal as her city. She had already snuck into some of the lectures of Berkeley's General Chemistry class, Chem 1A.

It took Ruth only seven or eight minutes to get home. *Home.* She held the word in her mouth. Soon, she'd move out and make her own home, perhaps a series of temporary ones. With a tightening throat, she realized she'd miss the building more than her parents.

She unlocked the door. As she pushed it open, she heard a male voice.

"What if the weapons end up in the wrong hands?"

Ruth froze in her steps. *A burglary? What am I supposed to do?*

"We'll just have to take that chance," another man said.

"We don't have to make that decision now." Her father's voice.

Something relaxed inside Ruth. Something else went colder. *What the hell?* She couldn't let them know she'd heard. Very slowly, she backed out onto the front step and closed the door. She stood there a few seconds, thinking. Then she put her key in the back pocket of her jeans and rang the doorbell.

Quick steps behind the door—her father opened.

"Ruthie? You're home early." He looked surprised, alarmed.

"Mr. Pestoletti's sick." Just now, she didn't want to examine her father's face. "I guess they couldn't find a sub. Sorry, I forgot my key. Where's Mom?"

"I was wondering that myself. I just picked up a couple of colleagues at the airport. I'll introduce you."

Ruth felt apprehensive. She hoped her face didn't show this. The two guests sat on the blue couch across the coffee table from Dad's chair: a middle-aged balding man with an expressionless face and a younger guy with a short haircut and a suit that fit him too tightly.

The room was full of light.

"Bob and Frank." Dad pointed at one man, then the other.

Both nodded. Frank was busy collecting paperwork from the coffee table and stuffing it into a brown leather briefcase.

"Nice to meet you," Ruth said.

Something about this scene was wrong—but what? As if the three of them had lost track of time and were embarrassed. Ruth was shaken up in a way she couldn't quite explain.

She headed up to her room. On her way through the kitchen, she grabbed a can of Coke from the refrigerator. Out of the corner of her eye, she noticed the three men still watching her, as if barely containing their impatience to be rid of her.

CHAPTER TEN

2002, SAN FRANCISCO

Ulrike has to drive around for ten minutes to snatch a parking space in this mutating area in SoMa where epochs seem to change right before her eyes, neighborhoods transforming from industrial suburbs into humming urban areas.

The sharp August day slaps pedestrians in the face with its ridiculously blue sky and its subtropical comfort. She is here to collect a debt from a non-paying client. An utter void in response to her emails and to her increasingly urgent phone messages confirms that the intention to pay is sadly lacking. So is Ulrike's income. *I should charge the dirty motherfucker for every minute I've spent trying to reach him.* She is prepared to introduce this notion if the conversation takes the wrong turn.

The client, William, a retired Boeing engineer, requested a *simple website* to promote his memoir. They agreed on a fee of $800, which was paid promptly. Later, William requested a shopping cart, a feedback form, a blog—and agreed to the additional hourly charges. Everything seemed to be going well. That was a month ago. These new features took time and added up to a balance of $900. Ulrike can't afford to give up that much.

With irritation, she gets out of her car and heads to William's apartment. Ulrike has met him once, at a nearby cafe. He paid for her cappuccino and a cookie. He was charming in a gruff way, even if his memoir was tedious and his plans of selling it online ludicrous. Ulrike has never mustered the dedication to read the entire book, just leafed through it, a long account of mundane events narrated to glorify an insignificant life by attaching it to the achievements of others. *Who am I to judge? A life story like William's may be precisely what the readers want: to identify with his predicament, to share the insignificance.*

William's building is tall and gray, its lobby facelessly modern. An abstract painting across from the entrance enhances this impression. The water feature is attractively lit, and there are enough plants to start a forest fire. *What is it about, really—all these plants everywhere, as if we, as a species, are nostalgic for our earlier, less civilized habitats?* Ulrike can do without plants. *Some quirkier, less generic modern art would have been better.*

The elevator confounds her as she discovers that the large black button on the right has no effect. The second button, a red one, must be Emergency. She walks over to the door that leads to a stairway, but the door is locked. The elevator appears to be her only option.

She tries the stupid, self-important button again—to no effect, as if the building were just a model, occupied by model people. *What the fuck am I supposed to do?* Ulrike's frustration grows as it dawns on her that she might be unable to get hold of William after all unless she's willing to camp right here in the lobby. *Is William even in town? I'm too desperate, that's the problem. I should've let go. Should've spent this time on the next fucking project.*

Ulrike is about to abandon the endeavor when the front door swings open. A man in his early forties enters, his expression inquisitive, then understanding. Something in his hand, a small card—he waves it before the elevator's control panel, activating the magic.

He gestures for Ulrike to go in first. "What floor?"

"Four, please."

He presses 4, then 3, and the elevator takes off. The guy seems relaxed; he gives Ulrike a small smile. The elevator is sterile and predictable, with mirrors in two corners.

"Thanks, by the way," Ulrike says. "You saved my ass."

He briefly examines her as if she were an incongruous creature.

"Have a nice day," he says before getting off.

Ulrike nods. *Hopefully, the ride down doesn't require a magic wand—otherwise, I might be stuck here like a Ra-fucking-punzel, long enough for my hair to grow.*

The fourth floor is as empty as the lobby was. The corridors diverge mysteriously, neutral and impersonal in their dark gray. The building's geometry seems intentionally complex. After a while, Ulrike locates the apartment, the ornate digits on the door indicative of a quirky and old-fashioned taste.

She rings.

For a while, nothing happens.

Ulrike holds her breath, her head tilted so her right ear has direct exposure to whatever sounds the apartment may betray. The faintest rustle; something small moving quickly or a large thing trying not to move. Shuffling steps. The door swings open as if William had rushed to it and turned the handle in one continuous move. He looks terrible, aged a century in less than a month. His thin face is covered with heavy stubble.

"Oh, you..."

He seems relieved rather than aggravated. *What if paying or not paying the web design bill is not his main dilemma right now? Doesn't matter. I need the money, no matter what William may be going through.*

"Yes, it's only me. Only a small German web designer girl. William, are you okay?"

"Oh, hell. You don't wanna know." He looms in the doorframe.

"I'm sorry. I've come to ask for your payment, please. I won't bother you after that. I really need it."

"You really need it. Of course, you do. I'm sorry. Come on in. I'll write you a check."

Is he just trying to lure me into the apartment? But I came here of my own will. In any case, William is old, and I'm a strong girl.

William gestures toward the living room; Ulrike enters. A half-empty vodka bottle waits on the coffee table. William heads straight for it and takes a big gulp. The living room is a minimalist space, all black: a TV, a couch, a chair—even the carpet is black—while the walls and the ceiling are white.

"Wow!" Ulrike reacts to the contrast.

William grins.

She sits on the couch. William looks around hesitantly and plops down in the chair, the vodka bottle still in his hand. He takes another sip.

"What happened?" It takes an effort to keep her voice neutral. This whole business of collecting her fee is freaking her out, even if she is not physically scared. *Wasn't he going to write a check? And now what? A conversation to go with it?*

"Nothing. Nothing happened." William's smile looks more like a bitter grimace.

For a moment, Ulrike doesn't know what to say. She stares at the man's inscrutable, downtrodden face. *What recollections are stored in that brain? What obscure Boeing memories that would make no sense outside the context?*

"You didn't return my calls. Or emails."

"No. I haven't checked my email."

"What's going on with you?" She stares into his reddened eyes —and it occurs to her that from inside her, it's difficult to tell what impression her own eyes are projecting: scared, supportive, or fucking indifferent like most automaton people's empty stares.

"It's my father, you see. My father. A heart attack. But you know what gets me? He was there for two weeks before a neighbor found him. Imagine that?" William stares at something in the empty corner of the room, just below the ceiling, as if his father's spirit had taken up residence there.

"Weren't you two in touch?" *A challenging question. Why am I always so awkward with people? I'm not insensitive. I just can't seem to read the clues quickly enough.*

Sometimes Ulrike blames the culture and the second language challenges—but she's lived in the States for eleven years, more than enough to acclimate, unless she is truly a thumb-sucking imbecile, which sometimes, just sometimes, she suspects herself to be.

"We were in touch." William is reflective, his hand on his cheek. "We quarreled a lot. Family stuff, you know. Let's just say ours was not a very happy family. My dad..." He is lost somewhere for a second or two. "But we got along fine, we did. I called him every month or so. We'd exchange postcards for Christmas."

"How old was he?"

"Eighty-eight. In the last few years, his body kind of went, but his mind was still sharp. I have not shared this with anyone, and I probably shouldn't, but what the hell. You asked." William hesitates. "My life has gone to shit, you know. My wife left me a year and a half ago. We hated each other anyway. You know how these things develop over the years. Actually, you don't know, you're too young for that. Anyway, I thought I was happy about the whole divorce thing, but the more I sit around here on my own, the clearer it is that I'm not happy at all. Not at all. And my dad..." His voice cracks. "Dad was the only person in my life, really. I didn't care for him too much, but he was there, up in Seattle, always happy to talk whenever I wanted. And now..."

After a while, the silence becomes uncomfortable. But she

asked, and now she is prompted to follow up. "Why did your wife leave you?"

Another stupid question.

"Half of our life was avoiding each other. The other half, trying to provoke each other. It wasn't as dramatic as all that, and it wasn't pretty. She was the strong one. She left. I would've put up with her for the rest of my life."

"Doesn't sound too different from me and my husband."

"Didn't take you for the married type. You should dump him before you end up like me."

"But he's a good guy; he treats me well. I might be the bad egg. Sometimes I don't understand myself."

"If you're not happy, you're not happy. A drink to unhappy marriages?" William hands her the vodka bottle. Ulrike hesitates—but what the hell; she accepts it, takes a swig. The burn in her mouth supersedes other sensations. The warmth spreads in her blood.

"To unhappy marriages." She hands the bottle back to William, who follows up with a generous gulp of his own.

1983, DRESDEN

It's seven o'clock. Ulrike and her mother are still in the kitchen. The light outside is subdued, the white walls have faded to gray. They keep going over the interrogation and what it meant, what it didn't mean, what it might have meant. Ulrike's mind swims, in deep overload. She wants to sleep, just sleep. But she can't. They have to wait for her father to share the unfortunate development.

A breadth of time passes. The lock's familiar click—Papa wears a dark blue sweater and a pair of gray slacks. His thin, long face, his strong chin, his gray hair—at forty-five, he is a good-looking man. But he looks tired, preoccupied. He takes in the scene, their worried faces.

"What happened?" He stands there, stranded in the middle of the kitchen.

"Papa. Oh, Papa. A Stasi was waiting for me by the school today. He took me to his office and asked me questions."

"Questions? About what?"

"You. He asked about you." Ulrike can't contain herself anymore. Sobs shake her.

"Me?" Her father doesn't sound surprised.

"He said you help smuggle people out to the West. And Uncle Franz is cooperating with them. What was he talking about?"

"To the West? Uncle Franz? This sounds ridiculous, Uli. It's nothing. It's *Zersetzung*. Don't worry about it."

"*Zersentzung?*"

"You haven't heard the word?" His eyes examine her with interest and admiration. "It means to compromise, to subvert. They'll tell you things about your family. They'll tell you that your family is already cooperating. That's how they trap people."

"Shouldn't we ask Uncle Franz?"

Her father shakes his head. "We'll talk to Franz, for sure—to warn him. These people will tell you anything, dear. This is how the Stasi operate. Nothing they say has any value."

A sense of relief makes a hesitant entry, but something about this relief doesn't connect.

"Why you, Papa? Why us?"

"You know how things are here. Someone may have reported us."

"Who could have reported us? Why would someone dislike us so much? We are nice people, aren't we?"

"I don't know, dear," Barbara pipes in. "Could be anyone." She sounds unconvinced.

"What should I do if Vogel comes to see me again?"

"Just tell him that he's a liar and you have nothing to say." Barbara looks vulnerable despite the bravado of her words, her jaw clenched under a worried frown.

"Correction." Her father smiles. "Don't tell him he's a liar. No need to challenge these people overtly. Just tell him you have nothing to say."

"Do you think he'll come back?" Ulrike feels a scared grimace where her face usually is.

"I hope not. I hope not."

He will, Ulrike tells herself. *He will*.

2002, SAN FRANCISCO

"I'm sorry about this whole website thing; I am." William looks embarrassed. "You did a beautiful job."

"Thank you."

Ulrike appreciates the black-and-white world around her. The contrast, the thought that went into it, the commitment to dealing with both extremes on a daily basis. She shouldn't be surprised: the website is also like this, per William's request.

"Just a moment." William looks around absent-mindedly. With some effort, he gets up and walks into another room, probably an office, with a corner of a cherry desk visible from Ulrike's position. Hopefully, he is getting his checkbook, and their entire business relationship can be put to rest.

One of the masks on the wall attracts Ulrike's attention. There is something sinister in the expression of its empty eyeholes, in the wrinkles of its wooden forehead. The mask is trying to tell her something indecipherable, all the while mocking her inability to understand. *William's life has gone to shit, and perhaps it's never been that wonderful in the first place—my own life fits the same description—and the mask knows this about both of us.*

William's return interrupts her thoughts. As he hands Ulrike her check, he holds something in his other hand.

"You know..." He smiles, but his smile is incorrect in a way Ulrike doesn't know how to read. "I was looking, you know... looking for my checkbook..." He pauses as if his thoughts had wandered. "And I found this." William shows the thing in his other hand—a gun, naked and real in the well-lit room.

What the fuck! The fear is intense and immediate.

Whatever happens will be her own fault. It suits her to be shot by a crazed Boeing builder rather than to rot away in her sad, predictable, immensely stressed life. Now she almost wants it to happen. It would be so easy. It would absolve her of so many responsibilities and so much guilt. In this brief pause, she straddles both states, holding tight to her existence and preparing to let it go. But William just hovers there with a gun directed at nothing.

"Oh-oh! No shit!" She finds herself speaking. "William, be a good host and put this thing away."

William seems to be listening, but it's impossible to read his face.

"You don't have to shoot me over nine hundred bucks. I'll tear up your check right now and leave, and no one has to know that any of this happened." She doesn't tear it up just yet; she's not ready for that. "You hear me? No need for a gun here."

William's face is red, his eyes ready to jump out of their orbits.

"Do you hear me?" Ulrike probes again. "Let's talk about it, okay? Okay?"

"Yes." William snaps into the conversation like a remote-operated toy, as if most of him were absent in a way Ulrike doesn't understand but is scared of. "My memoir is shit, isn't it? No matter how much I pay you." He leans on the door frame, the gun hanging barrel down in his loose hand. "I thought it would make sense, but the more I think of it, the less I like it. It's not easy to write a book. I thought I could just tell my story as it is, but the more I tried, the less I knew what my story was." Desperation rings raw in his voice. "Maybe all that crap I wrote is not really my story at all."

"Sorry, I haven't had a chance to read the whole thing yet. I can barely find time to get my own work done." In fact, she's never planned to read it; the book isn't even well-written.

William hovers pointlessly, his sad face lost in something resembling regret.

"Just shoot me and be done with it if you fucking must," she throws at him.

"Oh, fuck! Fuck. No one is going to shoot you. The check is yours. It's not about the money. It's not about anything anymore.

It's about..." William hesitates, an expression of intense thought on his face.

He seems to give up, his face relaxes, and Ulrike assumes that the worst has passed. Instead, in a move too quick to be unpracticed, he inserts the gun's barrel into his mouth and pulls the trigger.

Bright red explodes over the black-and-white room.

CHAPTER ELEVEN

2003

Ruth snoozed one too many times, and her morning routine ended up cramped into a mere twenty-five minutes. This didn't allow any time for pondering her predicaments. The tension during bagel toasting was palpable. The frightening letter, the fake ID, Ulrike, Peter's sadness—all of this incomprehensible stuff bounced around in Ruth's mind. She couldn't think.

Jingfei's happy face was the first thing Ruth encountered upon entering the lab. Her colleague had been coming in earlier each day as if trying to tidy things up so she could run off to her new happy ending. Ruth hoped Jingfei's happy ending was real. With everything so upside-down in Ruth's life, facing so much happiness at once was almost intolerable.

She waved her rigid arm in a sloppy greeting. Jingfei's face lit up.

"Ruth! Good morning! How are you?"

"Need some coffee." Ruth pointed her thumb toward the kitchen. A moment alone was what she needed.

"Sure. Sure. I just wanted to tell you this idea I had about the compound. Something we talked about last week. I've been thinking about it, and..."

"Not now, Jingfei! Can't you just give me a moment?" Ruth's voice came out impatient, irritated.

Immediately, the joy in Jingfei's face was extinguished.

In a softer voice, Ruth tried to fix it. "I'm really sorry, Jingfei. Just give me a moment, please. It's the stuff in my life, not anything to do with you or work. It's me. I'm so sorry. I just need some coffee."

Jingfei's face softened. "Of course, Ruth. I'm sorry."

"Thank you. I'll catch up with you in a few minutes, okay?"

"Take your time." Jingfei's small, elegant figure dressed in fitting jeans and a stylish blue blouse was already withdrawing.

Four days had passed since the letter, but Ruth hadn't decided what to do. She was scared. In the kitchen, the coffeemaker sat silent and cold. Jingfei was not a coffee person, preferring instead her exquisite collection of herbal teas, which she generously shared with others. Jingfei didn't get caffeine.

Ruth carefully poured the water. Her hands shook a bit. She opened several of the elegant, dark gray cabinets before she found the coffee.

When enough brown drops had collected, Ruth pulled the pot out with a gesture that came out exaggeratedly athletic, as if the pot weighed forty pounds. As a result of this awkward move, some of the freshly made coffee splashed right onto her light blue blouse, more on the floor. The steaming fabric clung to her skin.

"No!" She screamed.

It took Ruth a second to think of a simple move: to pinch the fabric and pull it away from her skin. No major harm done but for a gigantic coffee stain on the front of her blouse.

Jingfei was already there.

"Ruth, are you okay?" Such genuine concern on Jingfei's face.

"Yes. Just made a mess of myself." Ruth was relieved to find their interpersonal situation reduced to slapstick comedy.

"I have an extra T-shirt on my bench if you'd like to wear it. You're about my size."

"Really? Thank you, Jingfei. You're a lifesaver. I should keep one here as well. Never occurred to me. A brilliant idea."

"It would have come to you sooner if you were as clumsy as me." Jingfei's smile was tentative. "Ruth, I just want to let you know. If you ever want to talk about anything, I'm here for you. Like your family and things. But if you're not into that, no problem either. It's cool either way."

What a well-considered offer. "Sure. I appreciate it. You've heard about my father, right?"

"Yes. It's terrible. Terrible."

Of course, Jingfei had heard. Everyone in the lab had handed in their sympathy notes.

"I'm sorry. It's not one of my best days," Ruth said.

"That's okay. We all get days like this. Don't worry about it."

Ruth sighed. *If only it were that simple, not to worry.*

Soon, her coffee mug was in her hand. The incident in the kitchen was over. With Jingfei's dry shirt on, Ruth felt better, though she was ashamed of being rude earlier. She sat at her bench, sipping her coffee, not opening any documents or checking her email. The lovely bitter molecules.

Awaking from her stupor, she placed her fingers on the keyboard. The screensaver of the Bay Area's many beautiful spots was whisked away in favor of a standard, reliable desktop. Ruth opened her email and clicked *New Message.*

Dear Peter,

You probably didn't expect another email from me, and I'm not quite sure why I'm writing. I hope you're doing okay.

Everything seems very strange at the moment. I still think of Ulrike every day, but I don't know why. It's all mixed up with my father's death. I feel there is a connection, but I don't know what it is. Have I mentioned my father? He was killed by a BART train a few weeks ago. No one knows why. I can't figure out any of it. Maybe you feel the same? It's presumptuous of me, but would you like to meet again and talk? I don't mean to impose.

Ruth

Ruth reread the email. She couldn't predict how Peter might react. Her reasons for writing were unclear even to herself. She hoped she'd understand them better by the time she heard back. If she ever would.

If she hesitated any longer, she might never commit to it. She let the mouse hover over the Send button just a second or two before pressing it.

1986

Ruth sat on her bed, thinking. *Weapons? Could I have misheard? What the hell were they talking about? Financial weapons?* It would be awkward to ask Dad directly. But she wanted to ask.

What is Dad involved in? Ruth took a few sips of water from a half-full glass that remained next to her bed from last night. Her muscles felt tense; her hands shook a bit as she held the glass to her mouth.

Someone pulled on the door, found it locked, and knocked.

"Yes?"

"It's me." Mom's voice.

Ruth opened.

"What's going on, Ruthie? It's almost eight o'clock. You haven't left your room all evening." The martini glass in Linda's hand was half-empty. She liked to have an after-dinner drink around this time, her second. Her first came at varied times in the evening.

"Who were those people?"

"What people?"

"The two guys visiting Dad."

"Oh, I don't know, dear. You should ask him. I try to stay out of it."

"My god, why? You two are married. And you don't want to ask him who he brings home."

"Don't rush to judge, dear. When you're my age, you'll understand."

Ruth hated this empty guarantee.

Should I even mention the whole weapons thing to Mom? She would probably brush it under the rug. Ruth could hear her mother's voice in her head. "Darling, why don't you ask your father?"

* * *

"Dad, I heard you talking about weapons," Ruth blurted out one day over breakfast. She couldn't get it out of her mind.

"Weapons?" Her father's face was neutral—almost too neutral. "Who was talking about weapons?"

"You and those two guys who stopped by last week. Bob...Bob and..." Both names had been on the tip of her tongue, but now she couldn't remember the second.

"Frank. It was Frank. But what's this about weapons? You must have misheard. Honestly, I can't remember what we were talking about. We had a busy few days. Probably business strategy. How to best implement innovations."

Ruth tilted her head. *Innovations? What innovations?*

"Well...it just sounded strange, that's all." Ruth was hot from embarrassment. She couldn't quite meet his eyes and stared at her cereal instead.

She couldn't believe she was considering her father this way. She loved her father—her ally, a sensitive, considerate, slightly distant person next to her mother's self-immersion. He had his quirks, but they were benign. At least they'd appeared so, until now. She wished she'd had access to something like *truth*, something objective—not just her father's denial. She resisted having to change her opinion about him.

"I'm so sorry if something we said spooked you." Dad smiled encouragingly. "We didn't mean to."

A chill ran through Ruth. She didn't know whether his smile was sincere or not. *If weapons hadn't been mentioned, would I still feel suspicious? In the end, what do I know about Dad's life?*

There was no end to questions.

Ruth lay in bed, watching the play of lights on the ceiling. The city, an experiment forever ongoing. Sleep was not coming. For a millionth time, she asked herself if she should call Rodriguez and let him know about the threatening letter. *What about Ulrike's past in the GDR? It must have been a million times more unnerving than anything I can imagine. What would she do?*

Marie Curie would never hesitate to do whatever she felt was right. Marie came from a family of fighters for independence; she wouldn't care about the repercussions. 'Nothing in life is to be feared. It is only to be understood.' *If I'm to be a great chemist, I will have to overcome my pathetic lack of resolve.*

David Conrad—what a strange fake name: so generic. Ruth forced her body to relax and felt its weight on the mattress. The letter was her father's problem. She didn't have to make it her own.

It already *was* her own.

She'd been obsessively mining her memory for any unusual recollections concerning her father. Their walks involved several patterns with minor variations of blocks and street corners. Her dad would usually bring a newspaper. Sometimes a letter.

Yes, a letter, to drop into a mailbox.

Strange, with a mailroom at his office. Or was it? It had never occurred to Ruth to question this. *If Dad had to drop off a secret letter, why do it in front of me? That makes no sense. He had thousands of other opportunities.*

Has he done bad stuff too? Sending threats? She pushed this thought away. She was sweaty in her bed, lacking a comfortable position to settle in.

Would Dad call the police if he were in my shoes? If he were alive?

If only everything could stay still: the street, the apartment, my life. Still like that picture of Marie Curie driving her mobile X-Ray vehicle. In the picture, Marie looked resigned, as if war and radiation were common sense matters, even if they would eventually kill you.

And Ulrike? What was she like?

CHAPTER TWELVE

What the fuck! What the fuck! In Ulrike's ringing ears, the thud of William's body hitting the floor registers as an irrelevant, delayed addition to the gunshot sound. Her hands fly up to cover her mouth. She wills herself to move, pushes herself off from the couch, rushes toward William—but there is nothing, nothing at all to do. She can see the bloody gap where the upper left of his skull used to be. The blood covers the top corner of the door where William was leaning and descends like a morbid waterfall. A dreadful mix of smells reaches her nostrils. Ulrike retches and throws up, contributing to the horrifying variety of bodily liquids.

The red is especially distinct on the white walls, adding a sinister twist to the high-contrast look. Ulrike walks over to the window. *The cars and the pedestrians are so unaffected.* She takes a breath.

The check is still in her hand. She'll have to cash it as soon as possible. She is a bit ashamed of this untimely consideration. She glances at the check, and the number is $1,500 instead of $900. *Shit! A suicide tip?*

Fear of authority from years ago surfaces in her. *Any interaction with the police is a wildcard and might get me in trouble. I'm an immigrant. I could be deported.* She's tempted to run and leave it to someone else to report the suicide. But running off would make her a suspect rather than an unfortunate witness. Wrong place, wrong time.

William has paid up and then some, and she owes him at least this last honor: to report his death before his deteriorating body attracts olfactory attention, like his father's. Besides, the man in the elevator saw her, not to mention all the cameras. *Fuck! What in the world did I get myself into?*

I'm no longer in the GDR.

It's safe to call 911.

It's safe.

Ulrike looks around for a phone but doesn't see one in the living room. She enters the office, where the cherry desk, dumb and old-fashioned, takes up an exaggerated portion of space. Two desk drawers remain open, a grim reminder of the two actionable items William happened to pull out, the checkbook and the gun. With this thought, Ulrike folds the check and stuffs it into the back pocket of her jeans. She can't mention the check, or it may be held as evidence, and she'll never get to cash it. Her hands are shaking.

An old-fashioned rotary phone on the desk. Ulrike picks up the receiver. She forces herself to act and spins the phone's wheel with a long nine, the wheel struggling to make it home, followed by two concise ones.

"911 Emergency," a tired female voice says in her ear.

Ulrike is mute, paralyzed. *Where should I start? How does someone describe this: the gun, the blood, my reason for being here? What would the Stasi think? Maybe I should hang up.* She wills herself not to do so with every bit of strength she has.

"911 Emergency." More tension in the voice this time.

"Yes. Sorry. Yes, there's been an accident. Not really an accident. Suicide."

"Is the victim still alive?"

"No, no." Ulrike begins to cry.

"Please state your location, Ma'am."

"I'm...oh...I'm at a client's place. It's near Mission. I have the address in my notebook. I'm sorry. Hold on."

Ulrike nearly drops the black receiver and rushes back to the living room, where blood still leaks from the gaping absence in William's head. Her purse is on the couch, but when her trembling fingers open the clasp, the notebook is not there. Feverishly, she retraces her steps. It's still in the back pocket of her jeans where she stuck it after locating William's street address. Awkwardly, she pulls it out and runs back to the phone. She feels as if an hour had passed.

"I have it!" She's out of breath.

"Go ahead, Ma'am." The woman's voice is impatient.

Ulrike deserves this. She should have looked up the fucking address before making the call. She reads it off.

"Ma'am, we are sending a response team. Please identify yourself."

"Ulrike Schumacher."

"Please spell it," the woman says.

Ulrike does; one of a hundred times she will have to do it this year.

"Please stay at the scene until first responders arrive."

"I will."

Ulrike hangs up. Alone in this apartment with a dead body, she's not sure what to do with herself. It's not a situation she'd ever imagined herself in. *Should I have told the operator about the stupid elevator button? I should have, shouldn't I?* She's tempted to call back. *The police must have all kinds of ways to know about these things.*

Against her better judgment, Ulrike approaches the sprawled body, its grotesque head still oozing liquid, the blood invading the carpet's black, becoming less real. A surprised expression rests on what's left of William's face as if he were still intensely pondering his situation, working out a more practical plan. The broken edges of skull where the bullet came out are jagged and covered with slime. Nausea returns and Ulrike forces herself to abandon this spectacle before contributing any more of her own bodily emanations.

She checks the hall adjacent to the living room. The bathroom is small, dirty in a male way, with stains of urine and a few pubic hairs on the toilet's outer edges and a matching smell. She rests her arm on the counter, making eye contact with her scared reflection. Something red in her long hair. William's blood. Horrified, she turns the faucet on and bends low, bringing her hair under the tap. She rubs and rubs and rubs the affected spot. The blood smears, and worse, she finds something else in her hair, something small and sharp—a bone fragment. Disgusted, she tosses the nasty thing away and fits her entire head under the tap—and this is when the doorbell rings.

Scheisse. She should have unlocked the door. *Shit, shit, shit.* Her hands claw through the wet hair, trying to perform a minimal cleansing in just a few seconds. *What if they find William's DNA on me?* She's horrified—but the next second, she calms down, remembering she is not under suspicion. Still unsettled, she runs to the door, forgetting to turn the water off.

Two cops are at the door: a big guy, older, with gray hair, and a lady about half his size and age, but with a firm, practiced cop expression on her round face.

"I'm Inspector Rodriguez," the man says. "This is Detective Smith. Did you call 911?"

"Yes."

He takes in her hair, still dripping.

"I got some blood on it."

"What's your name, Ma'am?"

Ulrike replies without making eye contact. The man is annoying, one of those correct, official people she's had enough of in her old life in the stupid GDR. 'Authority figure' as they say here. *Now I'm in deep shit: I'll be implicated in some fuck-forsaken crime just for being here at the wrong time. The old guy will make sure of it.*

Rodriguez walks into the living room; Ulrike sheepishly follows. He examines the body and nods as if confirming a theory he has already formed.

"Can you tell me what happened?" Rodriguez's gray eyes return to her.

"I'm here...I came...just to get paid for a project. A web design project. Something I've done and delivered. I couldn't reach him, you see. I've tried for weeks."

"Slow down, Ma'am." A smile on the inspector's face, so incongruous at the moment that Ulrike immediately feels better.

Something about him reminds her of someone else, a secondary figure in her life, one with positive connotations. She can't quite grasp the memory—it could be a shadow of a story she's heard or read rather than her own life.

"Yes. Sorry." She tries to pause a little after each statement. "He told me about his father and his wife, and then he shot himself."

"I see."

Rodriguez gives a nod to Detective Smith, who begins an inspection of the suicide scene, taking pictures with an expensive digital camera and occasionally jotting down notes in a small pad. Rodriguez's eyes follow Smith for a few seconds, then return back to Ulrike. They stare calmly and confidently, without challenge.

Ulrike has to admit: the eyes are okay—something decent about them, as if he still finds a good reason to wake up each day. *Maybe I misjudged him at first?* It's not just the eyes, it's the way he asks his questions—softly and politely, indicating that he wants to know in the purest sense—for the truth of it, not for his personal goals or some such. *Still, some guys have it practiced, the nice guy act. The Stasi had it down cold. I have to be careful.*

"Were you scared?"

What a question.

"Yes. Yes, I was. But honestly, I didn't think he would shoot me. I thought he wanted to scare me. I'm sorry. I don't know. I'm not sure what I thought. It happened fast."

"How fast?"

Ulrike replays the entire depressing occurrence in her unlucky head. "He was talking about his book and how hard it was to write one. I just played along. Then he put the gun in his mouth, and that was that. It must have been ten, fifteen minutes."

"Very good, Ms. Schumacher." The inspector's gray eyes are calm and understanding, and his pronunciation of her name correct. "And now, please tell me everything again, step by step."

1984, DRESDEN

Ulrike steps through the large school door. As the winter air hits her face, she notices Vogel's car parked at the curb. Something clenches in Ulrike's stomach. She's had nightmares about this, hoping against hope that the Stasi would leave her alone. And he had, for over a year.

Vogel has spotted her, his gloved hand waving. If she ran, surely he would find her at home or back at school tomorrow. She hates the thought of hearing his voice again and, even more, the fact that she has no choice. In this country, she's not unique in having no choice, but there is no consolation in that.

She's only fifteen.

Snow falls lazily, melting soon after hitting the pavement.

Why wouldn't Vogel try a little harder to conceal his visit from other students and from teachers? The overt nature of this invasion must be precisely the point. Everyone is guilty in advance, liable to be next in line for the role of enemy of the state.

Now friends at school will act carefully around her. She will be considered an informer whether or not she agrees to collaborate. Stasi informers are everywhere. She'd probably be one of several in her class. No one knows for sure—except for the Stasi themselves, with the asshole Mielke at the helm.

Tales of Stasi prisons travel around: water torture, sleep deprivation, radiation tagging for released prisoners. But she's also heard of more subtle subversion. The Stasi will sneak into your apartment and reset the clocks, move your favorite chair—just to play with your head, to make you late for work, to unsettle you.

Her classmates may still be forming their idea of the Stasi based on the way their families deal or don't deal with the topic. Brigita's parents, young and apolitical, are more interested in hiking, sports, and sex. They don't have any opinions on the matters that preoccupy Ulrike's family. This is why Ulrike tries to educate her friend based on the discussions in their more critical household.

Thoughts spin like scared rabbits in Ulrike's mind, but Vogel is waiting. She approaches, a feeling of shrinking visceral as if all vitality had been sucked out of her. Vogel rolls down the window.

"Get in." He waves to the passenger seat like last time, clearly a gesture he employs often in his line of work.

He wears the same blue overcoat. At least it's appropriate for the chilly windy day. Ulrike walks over and gets into the car. The vehicle is well heated.

"You haven't called me." Vogel's face in profile is unreadable: not angry, not upset, not invested—a face turned off, a still prototype.

"I have nothing to tell you."

A small group of her classmates scurry by, their eyes briefly examining her situation, then quickly switching off to something in the distance. *Why am I stuck in this car with this horrible man while the rest of them get to run off home, read, play, do their homework, talk on the phone, feel safe?*

A subtle undertone of an unpleasant odor hangs in the car—not sweat, more like mold. *Is this what a Stasi car smells like? A Stasi life? A Stasi?*

"Nothing to tell me, *Fräulein* Schumacher? Really? Still protecting your father? I have to tell you that our file on him is almost complete. It's very strong. It gets better. Your mother is also involved. If both of them go to prison, who's going to take care of you? You'll end up in a children's home. Do you know what happens to girls in children's homes?" Vogel turns his head and looks at her squarely, his eyes cold and confident, a small grin on his lips. *He enjoys his work. He's a person without a person inside.* "I don't mean to be crude. I'm sure we'll come to an agreement." He softens as if already aware that his attack came out too strong. He's the bad and the good interrogator in one person.

Children's homes. Ulrike has heard about a girl raped by her children's home director, a rape she couldn't report. Other teenagers were humiliated and destroyed for reading foreign books or sharing their political concerns.

"You lied about Uncle Franz." She wasn't planning to challenge Vogel, but here she is, doing just that.

"I did? What is it you think I lied about?"

"He's not collaborating with you. He'd have nothing to tell you. You're wrong about my father." She piles one statement upon another. It's too late to slow down.

"Am I now? Well, well." Vogel's laugh is void of merriment. "Tell me, does your father often get home late?"

"No."

"No?" Vogel stares as if her answer were not only incorrect, but incomprehensible.

"No."

"And your mother?"

"No," she says.

It makes no sense. No one always comes home at the same time every day. People run late. They have plans, errands, and shopping to do. Just another question designed to make anyone, anyone at all, look guilty. A question should be an opportunity to explain rather than to entrap. Thinking things through in this way makes Ulrike feel stronger and more capable to face this man.

Today, Vogel doesn't seem to be planning to take her back to his office. He is happy talking right here, by the school building. The sandwich and Coca-Cola routine is not for today. At least they are out in the street. She won't be tortured.

"I have some pictures to show you." Vogel hands her a stack.

She flips through them: ten or twelve, all similar, good color photos shot on film much better than the domestic ORWO brand. Each picture, almost identical: a group of six or seven people, including her father, around a dinner table. A series of candid shots, but not hidden camera. Some of them talk among themselves, their faces animated—others face the photographer.

"Do you recognize anyone in these pictures?"

Is that a trick question?

Why would it be?

Why wouldn't it? Ulrike has to think quickly. It would make no sense to deny that she can identify her own father.

"Of course," she says. "Why do you ask?"

"Tell me who these people are."

"These people? My dad is the only one I know. I don't think I've ever seen any of the others."

"Really?" He pauses. "Would it surprise you to know that this gentleman here and here and here and in several other pictures is a known dissident conspiring against the state?" Vogel points his finger at the face. "His name is Otto Bauer. He's about to go on trial."

Dad must not have known.

He may have known.

The whole thing might be a total fabrication.

She doesn't reply.

"Think carefully and tell me if you recognize Otto Bauer," Vogel insists. "Just be honest, and the country will take care of you."

The man in the pictures looks friendly, pleasant, even handsome. Not threatening at all. And then it's clear to her: the accusation must be valid, after all. It would be just like Papa to do something magnificent and dangerous for freedom.

"Which one is Otto Bauer?" she asks.

2002, SAN FRANCISCO

"What's going on?" Peter asks. "You've been acting strange lately."

They are in the middle of their coffee and bagel routine. Sure enough, something about Ulrike's fucking mood must have already upset him. He holds a bagel's buttered bottom on the palm of his hand as if weighing its fate.

"Have I? It's this client of mine. He..." Somehow, she is still uncertain how to tell the gruesome story, the memory of blood on black and white fresh in her mind. Her fingers fold and unfold needlessly as if they had their own way of telling. It's too late to stop.

"He?"

"He killed himself." Ulrike nods several times for no reason.

"Wow." Peter puts his bagel down and gives her undivided attention. "I'm so sorry. It's awful. Why?"

Silence builds second by second as Ulrike holds on to her coffee mug, a red buoy in the middle of a vast ocean.

"I was there." Her voice sounds balanced, much more so than she feels.

"Shit! How? When did this happen?"

"Two weeks ago."

"Two weeks?"

"Yes."

"But..." Peter's clearly confused. "Why didn't you tell me earlier?"

"I don't know, I don't know. Fuck! It was too much, just too fucking much. I didn't know where to begin. I was overwhelmed."

"You couldn't tell me because you didn't know where to begin? Uli, sometimes I don't understand you. I have no clue what makes you tick. And it's sad, really. Part of it must be my fault. Tell me this: wouldn't you want me to let you know if something happened to me? Or would you want me to wait two weeks?"

Wrong question: I could wait two years for all I care. This is why being with Dietrich is so much easier: he doesn't pressure her for disclosure.

"I would leave it up to you to tell me on your own time."

The red curtains are infused with the morning's angle of light, contributing a pink overtone to the entire room.

"Yes, yes. The right thing to say. Have you told Sally?"

"I have."

Ulrike feels good about addressing the matter with Sally. She is being proactive, but Peter wastes no time to ruin it. "Somehow, I'm not surprised. You tell your shrink before you tell your husband."

This is wrong. She shouldn't be accountable for her sessions with Sally. But then, she's complicit; she should either share them or not. She chooses to share them selectively, an effective shield.

"It's different."

"Different? Of course, it's different." Now Peter is getting pouty the way he is liable to get in these stupid, ridiculous situations they seem stuck in. Debates about control, intimacy versus privacy—the expectations one places on a relationship without announcing them upfront, and surely as fuck without confirming them with the partner.

"I knew you would turn it against me, somehow," Ulrike summarizes. "You always do. This is why I was afraid to tell you."

"Bullshit. It's just a copout to make the whole thing my fault. And it's not a matter of fault in the first place. It's a matter of non-communication."

"Non-communication, my ass! I'm not accountable to you for every fact of my life." Ulrike storms off and slams the bathroom door behind her.

A dumb move, really: she'll have to come out soon. *I can't just camp in the bathroom like a girl-fucking-scout on glue.*

1984, DRESDEN

Ulrike unlocks the red front door. She's been looking forward to getting home. The lights are off; the apartment is dusky in the fading light through the window. Two months have passed since Vogel's visit.

Ulrike's mother awaits, stiff at the kitchen table, her face smeared with tears.

"What...what happened?"

"Your father...he was arrested." Barbara wears her elegant blue dress, an eerie match to the tablecloth.

"Arrested?"

Ulrike doesn't want to understand, but she does. The whole of herself is exhausted from these Stasi encounters, from her entire short life. And now something stiffens in her mind too.

"But..." How to express the feeling bubbling up in her? It's not exactly sadness—it's disbelief. "Is Papa really involved in all that people smuggling stuff?"

Barbara looks embarrassed. "He didn't share this with you. He couldn't. You would have been implicated. Now you understand how these things work."

"I wish you'd told me. At least I would've had a chance to prepare." Ulrike collapses into the chair opposite her mother. *So the Stasi was right after all. Vogel was more honest with me than my own parents. But can I really blame them?*

"Was he helping people get out to the West?"

Her mother just stares at her without confirming or denying it.

"It's a good thing to do, isn't it?" Ulrike is so confused about morals and priorities that she needs a grownup to confirm her assessment.

"I don't know, dear, I don't know. In this family, we believe in freedom. You know what we believe." Barbara pauses. "But our life is going to be different from now on, Uli." Tears roll down her cheeks. "I'm sorry about that."

"Poor Papa! What will they do to him?"

Ulrike, too, begins to cry.

CHAPTER THIRTEEN

2003

When Ruth walked in, Linda sat at their regular table at TJ's, a steaming cup of coffee in her hands. Linda got up to hug her daughter, an unusually exuberant gesture for this mother. She smelled of mouthwash under the smell of coffee. Ordinarily, they met every other week or so, but Ruth's father's death had thrown everything off. Linda had become elusive, reluctant to go out.

"Hi, dear. How are you?" A half-smile was plastered on Linda's face as if she didn't know how to proceed.

"I'm fine, Mother. Let's compare the letters."

"Yes, yes."

They sat. With slightly shaking hands, Linda opened her purse. She was impacted by this more than she was willing to show. She removed a standard-size envelope and took out a folded sheet, trading it for Ruth's, which had arrived in a large, page-size envelope.

When both women were done reading, Ruth laid the two letters on the table, side by side. They were, in fact, identical, word for word, except for *father* replaced with *husband*. 'And to ensure your daughter stays out of trouble' was the only other sinister difference.

"What a twist, if I may say so myself." Linda's face retained that uncertain half-smirk. "What a puzzle." Her eyes were red. She must have cried earlier, even if she wouldn't reveal her weakness to Ruth.

"A puzzle? Don't you feel we're in danger?"

"Danger? Oh, sweets, I don't know. I've thought about it some more. We're going to play along, aren't we? That old bastard. Do you know that I may have never married him if he hadn't gotten me pregnant? And I can tell you, he was not the only one dying to marry me. In those days…"

"I know, I know," Ruth interrupted. "It's all my fault. I've heard all this before."

"This is not what…not how I meant it, dear." Linda's face was firm as if to reinforce that she had meant it exactly that way.

"Okay, okay, mother. Let's get back to our situation here. What do we do?"

Linda wasn't listening. "I swear I had no idea what he was up to. I still don't. Can you believe that?"

Ruth scanned her mother's face to verify her sincerity. A difficult task. Ruth wanted to believe that her mother was not involved, but the relationship between Linda's statements and truth had never been clearly defined outside the changing parameters convenient to Linda at any given time.

"It doesn't make sense." Ruth's voice came out tense. "He had a fake ID, for god's sake. You must have noticed something."

Linda appeared to consider this. She stared out the window as if the answer were supposed to arrive in the wind.

"You father and I, we lived together more than forty years. After so long, you don't always keep track of each other. Someday you'll know what I mean." Linda pointed at the letter spread between them on the table. "When did you get yours?"

"A couple of weeks ago."

"And you didn't tell me anything." Linda's expression was not exactly accusatory—it was oddly neutral.

"I was afraid you'd freak out. The letter says not to tell anyone. You in particular."

"Nonsense, dear," Linda said. "These kinds of shenanigans may have been something your father was involved in, but they have nothing to do with me, and I'm not going to be scared for no reason."

"No reason? Seems like plenty of reason to me. You can decide not to be concerned for yourself if that's what you want to do, but you can't make the same decision for me."

Linda said nothing.

How annoying.

She took a large bite of her blueberry muffin and chewed it slowly and deliberately, like a piece of steak rather than pastry that melts in one's mouth.

"Wouldn't sending one to you first make more sense?" Ruth shrugged. "I don't get it. You'd be the one to have his papers at the house, not me out here." Ruth made a broad gesture with her arm as if to encompass the entire Outer Richmond.

"I don't know, Ruthie. None of this makes sense. I considered going through his things, his office. Couldn't force myself to do it. Now I don't even know." Unexpectedly, Linda teared up. "I'm not up to it. Might as well just leave it alone."

"What do you mean, leave it alone?" Ruth felt no relief from sharing this predicament with her mother. Linda was manipulative and unpredictable, everyone else a tool or a toy in her hands, her emotions subject to her own fine-tuning. "We should find the documents and then decide what to do with them. Don't you think we owe it to Dad?"

She finished her coffee and made a mental note to order another. The irony: she would much rather share this ordeal with her dad. And Dad was the one who had caused the whole thing, or at least allowed it to happen. Her dad, her sweet dad, with his nebulous, nefarious hidden life.

"Owe it to him?" Linda's face was firm, bitter, real—for once. "He hid god knows what from us, and now we're supposed to owe him something?"

Ruth took a deep breath. *The past is subject to reconstruction— it's developing, like the future. The world is a bundle of chemical reactions in our brains, causing us to interpret and re-interpret whatever we have encountered.*

"If we don't do anything, do you think these people will leave us alone?" Ruth brought her palms together before her as an improvised gesture of sincerity. What she wanted was reassurance, rescue. She wanted her mother to say *Yes*.

Linda said nothing.

"I just don't know, mother. I don't know who they are and what they want and what they're afraid of. I just don't know." The tears were coming back. Ruth was embarrassed to cry in front of her mother. Something about Linda's demeanor turned any display of weakness into an unfortunate compromise. "Let's just think about it for a moment. Was he a spy? A criminal? There must be something you noticed at some point. What about his business travels?"

"Ruthie, I've said all I have to say on the matter." Linda paused. A few heavy seconds passed. "What difference does it make, anyway? Whatever it was, it must've been something terrible if he couldn't share it with us. Some nasty business I want no part of. I don't want to know any more than I already do."

This abdication of curiosity troubled Ruth. So soon after Dad's death, her mother was distancing herself from him, despite half a life together. But then, Linda was all about distance.

"Okay, mother. I see you're not going to cooperate. Never mind."

"I need to use the restroom, dear. Too much coffee, I'm afraid." Linda was a little hesitant on her feet. Her gait was tentative, an elderly person's.

And then Ruth knew: it had nothing to do with age.

Linda had fallen deeply into drink fifteen years earlier and was out of control for several months before Dad checked her into rehab, which cost the family that year's vacation. The signs were fresh in Ruth's memory. The shaking hands, the barely perceptible unsteadiness, the overreliance on dental hygiene.

Both of their lives were falling apart.

"Mother!" Ruth cried out.

Linda stopped and turned around. "What's the problem, dear?"

"You're drinking again!" Luckily, the place was deserted. No one cared about their small confrontation.

"Oh, no. Not really." Linda waved her hands before her defensively. "It's just these few days, just a drink or two. A drink or two, that's all."

"Mother, you know that's how it always starts. A drink or two. We've been through this before."

"Oh come on, Ruthie. Give me a break. My husband is dead, and my whole life was who knows what kind of goddamn lie. And I can't have a drink? Don't you worry: I've got it under control, I promise."

Ruth felt defeated. Her mother was on a slippery path—perhaps more slippery than Ruth knew. Ruth had no energy for this. Linda was a grownup, after all. Everyone had the right to grieve in their own way.

1988

Ruth sat on the floor in her small Berkeley dorm room, chatting with her roommate Sarah, a lovely and energetic Black student from LA. Slightly chilled, December air infused with light flooded the room through the open window. Sarah walked about as she talked, periodically casting a shadow on Ruth.

The two girls had been careful around each other at first, as new roommates tend to be: observing instead of challenging. But their views had turned out to be similar. Despite plenty of differences in their backgrounds, they believed in the same notions of fairness and equality.

Black kids in Ruth's class had mentioned the issues their families faced. She'd been reading Toni Morrison and James Baldwin, among others. Although racial segregation had been outlawed for more than twenty years, she knew that racists were alive and well.

It hadn't taken long for their caution with each other to subside, for their conversations to get substantial.

"How sad is it when a CIA Director becomes President?" All that delightful sarcasm in Sarah's expressive voice. George Bush had been elected the month before; few in San Francisco were happy about it.

"It's 9 out of 10 sad. At least he voted for the Civil Rights Act. He's better than some."

"Which doesn't say much." Nervous energy emanated from Sarah's every pore. She looked tiny in a tight pair of black jeans and a tank-top—perhaps 100 pounds, perhaps 90, her hair extra short— but she carried enough fire and energy for ten people. It was easy to like her. After all the avoidance and vague answers in Ruth's family, Sarah's directness was refreshing.

"Bush. A difficult last name to live with if you're a Republican."

The girls cracked up. Ruth was delighted that her dumb joke had worked.

CHAPTER FOURTEEN

2002, SAN FRANCISCO

Sally's lobby is a little more neutral than a person with a functional brain prefers, but it must match the clientele's average preference, which means the average of everything or exactly nothing. The large building is shared by several therapists, a setup Sally tolerates. Two generic brown couches are positioned at a discreet angle so that clients don't have to face one another, even though the only person Ulrike has ever encountered is an elderly woman who comes to see Sally's colleague across the lobby.

Sally opens her door and smiles her friendly shrink smile. Sally's office and her red couch are a whole other look—this contrast contributes to the sense that their interactions here are meaningful and that Ulrike's life will improve. Has it improved during the four years she's been seeing Sally? Hard to say—but she has someone to talk to, really talk, someone to keep track of her life.

Soon, the greetings are over, and Ulrike's usual mug of tea is grasped tightly in her hands.

"Is there something you would like to start with?" Sally offers.

"Yes." Ulrike's hands on the mug are stuck, powerless. "I've had some nightmares about the suicide. That's to be expected, but..."

Sally lets a moment elapse.

"But?"

"That's not what I wanted to talk about. It's the suicide itself. How do I make sense of it? Not that it's my job to make sense of it, but somehow it feels like my job, or at least something that might help. I don't know. *Scheisse*. I'm not suicidal or anything—we've talked about it. But logically, I understand William's move. What's the point in sticking around if life feels like stinking nonsense or a perpetual struggle?" Ulrike pauses to sip her tea. "But that's not it either. What I'm trying to figure out is: why did he have to do it right in front of me?"

Sally pauses meaningfully; she looks deeply invested in Ulrike's struggle. "What do you think?"

"Well, I don't have the fuckingest clue. If I tried to off myself, I would do it alone, so no one had to deal with it. Take poison or something. No clean-up, no blood. To do it the way he did it, you have to be someone who likes to show off, right? A narcissist? But I've read parts from his book, and the more I think of it, the less he seems like a narcissist. He sounds like an honest guy stuck in a boring life. He's even compelling somehow—but I might be saying this only because he blew his brains out right before my eyes. I mean, not the most considerate gesture, right?"

"A demonstrative one, yes. And a very violent one, against you." Sally's face tightens as if her muscles reacted directly to the gravity of this discussion.

"Violent?" Ulrike thinks a moment. "Yes, that's true."

"Last time, you said that the whole act may have been a spur-of-the-moment thing. Do you still feel this way?"

"How could it be otherwise? He didn't know I was coming. It's not like he had all day to plan a suicide to impress me."

Sally shakes her head. "He must have at least considered killing himself. The plan was there, ready in his head. The gun was in his desk, wasn't it? You didn't bring it. You just happened to be there." Sally is acting more opinionated than she tends to be.

Dear Sally, she must feel strongly about this.

"Would he have done it if not for me? That's the question I can't answer. No one can. The check, the tip, the gun, all that stuff. He must have known he was going for a bit of self-lobotomy when he added the extra money to the total. Was it for my participation in the show? Or was the extra money just a reimbursement for having to track him down? Shit, you can slice it so many ways. But the bottom line is: if I hadn't shown up, the dude would still be alive and well. That's what gets me most, you know?"

"I'm not so sure he'd be alive and well. In any case, you can't blame yourself for something someone else did." Sally's face is firm. "You were just a witness. Any complicity is unfair and unearned. Do you see my point?"

The swaying tree outside reveals and hides segments of electric lines, stealthy snakes in the leaves. Life would be so easy if one could abdicate responsibility at will. Back in the GDR, everything was everyone's responsibility, which meant no one's.

"I see your point. I do." Ulrike says. "But how can I discard William's head exploding three yards from me? The fucker didn't even leave a note. How could he? I didn't give him the time with my stupid check. And now, what am I supposed to do? In the book, he tells a story that's sticking with me. It's about this other engineer hired to help him. William had been working on a project, something to do with improved wing flexibility, way over my head. And it just wasn't coming together. Models kept breaking, stuff like that. But the new guy had an idea just a week or two after he was hired. The issue was solved right there and then. Not a huge deal by Boeing standards, just one of the many tasks for one of the many teams. But for William, it was a personal slap on the face, something to confirm that he wasn't exceptionally brilliant, that others right next to him were better at the same job. It's got to be difficult, don't you think?"

Ulrike ponders her own question for a second and sips her tea.

"How is it for you?" Sally shifts in her chair—now her right leg is folded over the left. "Who do *you* compare yourself to?"

The question hits Ulrike like a ton of rocks.

"It's different for me as an immigrant, especially an immigrant from such a backward, hopeless place. I always feel I'm worse at everything, especially talking to people and convincing them that I'm the right choice to do a project. No wonder I seem lacking in confidence. Fuck! I happen to think I'm pretty good at my job. Anyway, to finish the story, William's assistant was matter-of-fact about it and didn't boast or make a big deal or even mention it, but William could never get past that; he always felt awkward next to the guy as if he had revealed something about William that should have stayed hidden. And a couple of years later, the assistant got transferred to another location, and that was that."

Ulrike's eyes wander over to the tree and its dance with the electric lines, an ongoing play void of meaning. *What about the other clients who use this seat during the rest of the day, the same view before their eyes?*

"The assistant probably envied William for his ideas on other projects," Sally says. "Skills that William took for granted. I wonder if the assistant respected him more than he knew."

This thought is so unexpected that Ulrike laughs—involuntarily, as she tends to do when a statement overwhelms her with its completeness and its beauty, not only its humor. *Completely fucking plausible!* These minor epiphanies inaccessible to Ulrike on her own are one of the reasons why working with Sally is so illuminating.

"In the same way," Sally says. "Some of the stories you've shared lead me to believe that people respect *you* much more than you give them credit for. Maybe you are a little bit like William?"

1985, DRESDEN

The school's recreation hall is murky and generic. The life-affirming nonsense of hundreds of voices merges into a hum penetrated by the occasional high-pitched note. A flock of girls have gathered around Lotte, who has a newspaper in her hands. The girls pass the newspaper around, reviewing the front page.

Ulrike is curious. She approaches the small bunch and smiles at the others, but Lotte pulls the paper out of another girl's hands and makes a show of folding it and stuffing it into her backpack.

"Schumacher! I hear you're not safe to be around anymore." A smirk cuts all the way through Lotte's stupid face.

It's as if I've already been declared a Stasi collaborator. "Nonsense," Ulrike replies.

"Really? That's not what I've heard. Come on, girls, let's talk somewhere where we can have more privacy."

Some of the girls giggle. Ulrike's former pal and math study partner, Irma, casts her an embarrassed glance as she follows Lotte. Something empty grows inside Ulrike, like numbness, but without numbness. *To think that I used to respect this cow, with her enormous boobs hanging on each side like balloons. No wonder boys are crazy about her. Those brain-dead monkeys.*

Lotte is the first to overtly express her suspicions, but Ulrike has noticed others acting odd around her or staying away altogether. *All these visits from Vogel must have had their desired effect. Vogel. I should bring a knife and stab the guy.* She'd feel no pangs of conscience on his behalf.

2002, BERKELEY

The ceiling is white over them as they lie, relaxing after sex. Berkeley is quiet, comfortable, progressive, the best this cool new life of hers has to offer. Ulrike sighs, absorbing the cheerful light through the window.

"You never tell me anything about your past." Dietrich's voice is not challenging, just matter-of-fact.

"What would you like me to tell you? I don't even know where to start."

"Let's see. What's your favorite childhood memory?"

What a cliché question. Something to write a third-grade paper on. Ulrike stares into the vast open field of herself and finds it empty of answers. *Favorite? What does favorite even mean: the most important, the sweetest, the fuckingest, as in best orgasm ever? The question is simplistic, like Dietrich himself, but shouldn't I have something to say in response?*

"When I was about eight or nine, we'd go to this lake near Dresden. The whole family would come: Mama, Papa, and my uncle Franz. He was in a wheelchair, have I mentioned? Not many people had cars, but he was able to get one sometimes, somehow, which was absurd because he couldn't drive it himself. My parents would help him into the back seat next to me. My father drove. I don't even know how he learned to drive. I don't remember what the lake was called. We stopped going in the later years. It was the Stasi thing, you know." Ulrike stops, digs inside herself for the beginning and the end of the Stasi story, and decides not to elaborate. "We would just drive for a while. Two hours maybe. My uncle...he wasn't a talkative kind."

"Is he your dad's brother or your mom's?"

"My mom's."

Dietrich lights a cigarette and hands it to Ulrike. He lights another, and there they lie, facing the big fucking empty space of the ceiling. For a while, they don't talk, small wisps of smoke merging in the air above them, a parody of romance.

"Did he and your dad get along?" Dietrich asks.

"Usually. Unless my dad was late to pick me up, which was not infrequent."

"*My* uncle is a pain in the ass." He moves to drop the ashes into an ashtray on the bedside table.

Dietrich's uncle, my uncle! Even fucking Santa must have an uncle or two. Ulrike has trouble staying interested. *Why does the past matter if it's a burden we carry about, hoping to find some big meaning in it but finding just weight?*

Her cigarette is overburdened with ashes, but she doesn't have an ashtray on her side of the bed, so she must lean over Dietrich to reach the one he has commandeered. *Selfish asshole.* As she awkwardly proceeds about it, her breasts brush against Dietrich's chest, and because she had not planned it as an erotic touch, the dude's chest feels like a log, an obstacle, an inanimate object. She has to push herself up with her left arm to make the reverse maneuver; again, it's awkward. Her shoulder muscles barely make it. *Why am I so weak all of a fucking sudden?*

"Come on, get this thing where we can both reach it," Ulrike commands, and Dietrich places the ashtray on his chest where her breasts just were.

He asked her about her best memory, and the whole story has morphed into a trivial uncle discussion. *Clearly, Dietrich is not interested—and why would he be? Our entire relationship is based on mutual disinterest. But if he's not interested, why bother to ask?*

And who the fuck am I to judge? How much interest have I shown the world lately? A guy killed himself before my eyes, and I was there only to claim my slice of the stupid pie, the $900 worth of a shitty website for a shitty book. But she is reading the book now, and it no longer seems shitty. It's sincere and sad the way Ulrike's art is supposed to be if she ever manages to tear her ass from the metaphorical couch.

Ulrike makes an effort to push the cynical thoughts away. She closes her eyes to recapture those car rides with her parents and Uncle Franz. "The lake was nothing spectacular, but it was a lake. We didn't have things like lakes in our daily routine."

"You guys had a crazy life."

Such a nonsensically simplistic summary. "Crazy? You could say that. Something sincere about it too. Like going to the lake. Or having a life despite all that totalitarian shit, the propaganda."

"What was the worst thing?"

What a question—how to answer this in a sentence or two about a society rotten to its dumb-ass Honecker-infected ideology-saturated core.

"Some kids went to these youth camps—youth concentration camps, really. Hard labor. Not everyone knew about them, but for the worst infractions, our parents would threaten us, *You'll go to Torgau for saying things like this.*" More than an inch of ash hangs off the end of Ulrike's cigarette, and she shifts it toward the ashtray, taking care not to drop any on Dietrich's chest.

"Hey, you want a beer?" he asks.

"No, thanks."

Ulrike extends her right arm and puts out her cigarette, vehemently rubbing its end into the ashtray's transparent surface. For a moment, she imagines the ashtray gone, Dietrich's chest in its place. *Such a lovely chest to put a cigarette out on. Dietrich, with his beer and his superficial questions. The cigarette might make a hiss, cause a nasty smell of burning flesh.* The Stasi practiced this technique, even if they never officially acknowledged it. She, herself, has not experienced it. Neither has her father—not as far as he's revealed.

Ulrike's teeth are clenched together like pliers. She tries to relax her jaws. Being with Dietrich is like being with herself, except for *sex. What is it with the sex? Peter's available, and even when Peter's at work, there are plenty of utensils to do the job without wasting nearly as much time. It's the human thing, isn't it? The need for approval.*

She is compelled to keep talking, not only to share her memory but to convince herself that her low opinion of Dietrich is a mistake resulting from her own small-minded, dismissive attitude. "Anyway, it was a weird life, that's for sure. You always feared something: something you might say, something someone else might say about you."

"How did it get set up that way?"

"It happened after WWII when Germany was split up. That's what the fucking Russians did to us after doing it to themselves. Hey, the irony is that Germany has recovered fairly well, even East Germany, but the Russians are still fucked."

"Sure sounds like it."

"Do you have a memory like that?"

"Sure." He smirks. "My dad broke my nose when I was seventeen. I was eight minutes late to work at his damn store."

"Sorry, dude. Was he always that way?"

"He was a jerk. This was an extreme case, though. I'd been late a few times; that much is true."

"That's not a reason to break someone's nose."

"No, it's not." Dietrich exhales a cloud.

"Did you ever forgive him?"

"A little, at the end. He died a few years ago. Anyway, tell me more about the lake."

How ironic. Dietrich actually wants to hear more.

"Right, the lake." She closes her eyes to remember. "The water wasn't blue, no. More like dark brown. It must have been polluted as a witch's ass. A factory was just across on the other shore. The tall white pipes and everything, the streamlined, utilitarian industrial architecture. Like in Antonioni films with their decaying industrial landscapes upon which the characters' ordinary lives decay as well."

"What films?" Dietrich scrunches his face.

"Never mind. Let's focus on the lake. It's been so long I can't be sure I'm accurate. We'd stay just a few hours. You'd think after all that driving you might stay the whole day. It had something to do with Uncle Franz's medications. I would tune out the grown-ups and listen to strangers, birds, and kids in the water. I'd swim like a monkey and enjoy the sun." Ulrike pauses momentarily to decide where to go with this memory. "Sometimes my parents argued. My uncle didn't usually say much. He brought a book. Always something serious and grown up. Once, I remember, they brought a bottle of champagne, but may god strike me stupid if I remember what they were celebrating. The whole trip was brown somehow. You don't see that kind of brown around here. Not that we realized it then. To us, it was just *our world*."

"That sucks."

"Hmm...yes."

"I'm glad you made it out. Was it difficult to get a green card?"

"For a while I went to school. I ended up marrying Peter. Otherwise, I might've needed a work visa."

"So you married Peter to stay here?"

"I was going to marry him anyway. I liked Peter. I thought I loved him. I think I loved him. I still like him. Shit, I don't know. I can't explain. If I could, do you think I would be here? Fuck! Give me another cigarette."

Dietrich obeys and helps himself to one. For a while, they smoke in silence, like in Antonioni films.

"How long did it take to get your citizenship after you two married?"

"Four years and two interviews."

"No shit?"

"No shit."

"Why stay married to the dude if you don't care for him so much anymore?"

"I don't know. I've been thinking about this for a long time. He and I, we have a routine. It's a ship. It's on a course—some course, who knows where the fuck to, but that's no different for others. You can't just stop. You'd need a better option. By which I mean, *I* would need a better option. It's not like you're in a rush to marry me, motherfucker. Not that I would ever marry *you*."

Ulrike half-expects Dietrich to claim that he would gladly do so should she leave Peter, but no such claim arrives.

"Bitch." He laughs instead.

"Just the way you like me, asshole."

1985, DRESDEN

The apartment is quiet. Her mother must be out. Another letter from her father awaits on the blue kitchen table. Papa's been in prison for eight months. The letters are neutral, almost identical, lacking detail as if he were being held in a white room with no furniture and no discerning features. At first, Mama didn't share the letters, fearing that their bland emptiness would have an upsetting effect. Then it became clear that even a letter void of passion and detail was still a message, a thread. Barbara relented.

"The letters are censored," she explained. "He'd get himself into more trouble if he tried to *really* tell us something. Himself, and us too. He can't say anything. Poor man." Tears welled up in her eyes.

With her father out of the picture, distance is growing between Ulrike and her mother. Another thing Ulrike has learned during these two years is that friends don't help when you're in trouble. Indeed, their parents' group of friends, previously a lively, gregarious bunch of a dozen or so, have dispersed—all but one, Dora, a quiet single lady.

"I'm so grateful for Dora," her mother often says. "She ended up much more insightful and compassionate than anyone had given her credit for."

Ulrike sits at the kitchen table, her father's latest correspondence in tiny handwriting on a small sheet of paper before her. 'I'm well. Don't worry about me. They feed us well and don't bother us much.' Is this report accurate, or simply an obligatory comment? If he were tortured, if he were suffering, he wouldn't be able to share that. The episode at school comes back to her. *I'm not going to care. People are fair only when no risk is involved. To be okay in life, I must become self-sufficient, happy on my own.*

CHAPTER FIFTEEN

"What do you want from me, really?" Peter asked.

Ruth had expected a challenge. Peter's face had been gloomy since the moment she'd arrived at Saint Frank's. He avoided eye contact. They'd exchanged a few superficial remarks. Peter was a reluctant compound unwilling to engage in a chemical reaction. He had all the good reasons to feel that way. The café's formal beige coolness weighed on Ruth like never before. She took a sip of her cappuccino—such a helpful thing in this tense conversation, a way to buy a few seconds while she considered a response.

"I'm sorry, Peter. I don't know how to answer this." *I can do better than that.* Her fingers played with an unopened package of Sweet and Low someone had left on the table. She detested sweetened coffee. "I feel as if there's more to uncover. I realize this may sound odd. Do you always know what you want from every encounter?"

"That's ridiculous. Of course, I do." He seemed to consider this for a second, his face sincere and somehow endearing. *Being rude or inconsiderate is not his style.* "You've insinuated yourself into my wife's tragedy like it's your own thing—but it's not. Nothing about it belongs to you. You just happened to be there, that's all. That's all."

Insinuated myself? Ruth felt a sincere pain for Ulrike who shouldn't have died that day, whose death was a mistake, a wrong that should be righted. Even if it couldn't be righted, Ruth felt she had to try.

I wish Peter cared more.

Immediately, the thought horrified her. How wrong to accuse Peter of not opening up to her, a total stranger. *Who am I to judge his grief?*

"You're right. You'd be justified in walking away." Ruth imagined Peter's athletic figure rising and sliding away without another word. Instead, he scrutinized her intensely. "I don't know why this tragedy has affected me so much, and I have no idea at all if my unreasonable suffering over Ulrike's death is of any value to you or just another annoyance when you're already low. My father's death is part of it, you see."

Ruth had promised herself not to talk about her father. And here she was, blabbering away. *I'm hopeless.* But her tongue and her vocal cords raced at full speed, her brain seemingly uninvolved. "I just don't know anymore. As if I've lost the grip on reality. It had never happened to me before." She wanted to tell Peter about the terrible letter, but the moment didn't feel right. The words did not come out.

Would Peter think she was trying to buy his attention by parading a charade of sorrows before his eyes? If he did, what would it matter? All of these notions were so imprecise, too intangible to be understood, classified, and enumerated. She teared up. This happened often these days.

"I'm sorry about your father's death," Peter said, flatly.

His face was rigid, and Ruth knew why: this was sympathy he was unprepared to give, something she had forced out of him. She felt destroyed. It was good to give herself permission to lose it.

And lose it she did, muted sobs escaping her even as she did her awkward best to keep her outburst at low volume. An elderly lady in a white hat observed her compassionately, seemingly on the verge of tears herself. Something about it made Ruth even sadder. More vulnerable in sharing the sadness she had stored over these last few weeks, few years. Her whole life.

Peter watched Ruth with rigid care. She rifled through her purse for a tissue but couldn't find one. She used a napkin to blow her nose. How embarrassing to fall apart like this.

As she struggled with the napkin, Peter concentrated on his tea. Ruth noticed his miniature cheesecake and was mad at herself for not getting one. She laughed at herself internally for being so childish.

"What happened?" Peter's voice was tense. "You said he was killed by a BART train."

"I don't know. I don't know how it could have possibly happened unless he jumped or was pushed." She paused, her hand over her lips. "Enough about my father. I wanted to talk about Ulrike."

"What's there to talk about? What did you want to say?" Peter sounded puzzled rather than annoyed. "You didn't know her. This whole thing must be about you, not her." Something in Peter's eyes had softened.

Unexpected, but unexpected things happened all the time; the world was filled with them. Even atoms were irrational, electrons hesitant in their indeterminate states.

"I don't know," Ruth said.

"I didn't think so." Peter smiled a distant kind of smile. "These things are difficult to talk about." He thought for a while, looking away. "I mean, difficult to talk about without sounding cliché. I understand you don't have an opinion about Ulrike, it's more like having a feeling about the accident. Like it moved you. I don't want to shut it down. I'm sorry. None of it makes sense to me, either. I'll admit: it took me some time to decide to see you again." He paused and took a sip of his tea. "The truth is, I don't have anyone else to discuss her death with. I told a friend, but it didn't feel right. He's already in my camp. It's as if he's obligated to support me in every way. He'd already been critical of Ulrike because of some of the stuff that went on between us. But you—you are objective. Objective? Is that the right word? Distant." He sounded sincere and generous in offering her an opening.

"Thank you for saying this. It's as if I'm different now. This event is part of me." This hadn't occurred to Ruth until the words left her mouth. "Life has gained gravity. I feel like the lighter part of me is gone."

"I hope that's temporary." Peter's face had become even, pleasant. "The way you were affected by Ulrike's accident might have something to do with what's already going on in your life, specifically your father's death. That makes sense."

It does, when stated confidently by someone else. "I can't help feeling that I was there for a reason. But I'm a scientist; I don't believe in fate and things like that." Ruth was rambling, her hands cumbersome, grasping each other in the air and letting go, expending small calories of nonsense. "All this death, and then the threats. I haven't told you about them."

"What threats?"

"Mom and I both got these letters." Ruth narrated the text she remembered almost by heart. "The whole thing sounds like a conspiracy, except it must be real because my father is really dead. Apparently, he was a spy of some sort. Shit! I just don't know what to think."

Ruth felt terrible for taking over the conversation with her own story. Peter was dealing with so much more. *How would it feel to lose a partner rather than a father? And so young.* Ruth's thoughts were going down a rabbit hole. She forced herself to focus.

"That's terrible," Peter looked genuinely concerned. "What did you do?"

"Nothing yet. I don't know *what* to do."

"It sounds like a movie."

"Right. I thought it may be a mistake. But how could it be? The letters are addressed to the two of us."

"Are you going to call the police?"

"I just don't know if I'm willing to risk it, that's the thing. And why should I? I don't know what the stakes are. Why should I take them on? This business has nothing to do with me. Just some crap my dad did."

It felt good to talk frankly to a human being who was real and friendly and a little distant. Ruth's plan to distract him with her troubles was working.

"What was your father like?" Peter really was quite charming.

"He was kind. Attentive." Ruth had not prepared a quick summary. "He listened. He remembered. He kept track of our stories. His smile is what I remember most. He'd always smile at us, Mom and me. Except for the times the two of them were fighting, which was pretty frequent."

"What did they fight about?"

"Minor stuff. Anything came in handy to start an argument. Not all families are that way, are they?"

"Ulrike and I had our better days and our worse days. But my parents—my adoptive parents—are very straight, religious. They are the kind of people who follow the rules. Conflict is not their style. I love them, I'm grateful to them—but frankly, there are few matters on which we agree."

Ruth enjoyed watching Peter's face as he said this. Most people obfuscated their life stories.

"Do they live here?" she asked.

"Sacramento. I escaped as soon as I could. But I'm forever grateful to them for adopting me. I didn't mean to sound as if I'm not." That cute wrinkle on his forehead when he thought about something significant. A smart face. "And your mother? Is she here?"

"Yes. I was born here in the city. Most people are from someplace else, aren't they?"

Peter's expression was so alive the face itself seemed to think before Peter said or did something. "Since you mentioned fights, Ulrike and I had a fight that day, just a few hours prior to...to her death. And I can't help blaming myself. You see, I got her a cellphone. Everyone at the office got an upgrade, and they offered a free one for partners and spouses. Anyway, she ran off. I tried to call her, to apologize. She..." Peter paused for an eternal moment. "She never picked up."

Ruth was tense, uncertain how to react. She could feel a frown of hesitation on her face. She sipped her cappuccino without taking her eyes off Peter as if he were still speaking. He looked away.

"What did you two fight about?" She realized she'd repeated Peter's earlier question about her parents. Fights and their causes defined the world.

"Nothing. Logistics. Finances. How to treat each other. I can't even remember half of what we've said when we were fighting. Isn't that horrible? After a while, even fighting becomes a habit, becomes forgettable. Ulrike..." he broke off.

"Ulrike?"

"In some way, I don't understand fighting. I don't know how to do it right. It makes me physically uncomfortable."

"I feel the same way." Ruth paused.

She expected Peter to continue, but he looked at her as if waiting for her to say something.

"So you worry you may be responsible, because of that cell-phone?" she asked. "But she didn't pick up, did she?"

"Maybe she was trying to get it out of her purse."

"That's just a theory. We'll never know what really happened." *The unsettling truth.*

"Sometimes I wonder if she may have...you know...done it on purpose. She was on anti-depressants. She had it under control. But..." He disappears, his stare somewhere deep inside his own destroyed life. "...but she had seemed strange lately. Well, she always seemed strange. This was one of the things that made her interesting. I don't have a clue, you see. Can I tell you something? It's kind of shameful."

"Of course."

"It's been over a month, and in so many ways, it feels..." Peter closed his eyes, as if to verify what he was about to say. "I feel more balanced, somehow. I also cry for her almost every day. How can this make sense? I miss her terribly. But day to day, things are easier without her negativity. She had two modes, attentive and sarcastic. That's a simplification, sure, but bear with me. Often, she would just make fun of something important to me. I don't get any of this yet. I don't know what made her do that. I feel I was only beginning to understand her. Absurd, isn't it, after you spend six years with someone?"

"It doesn't sound absurd." Ruth shook her head.

"Sorry to bother you with all this drivel."

"You're not bothering me, Peter. I want to know. I'm the one bothering you, remember? I was the one who reached out. I'm so stuck with my fear and the simple compounds at the lab. People make so much less sense."

"Yes." Peter seemed lost in his thoughts again.

Ruth sat straight in her chair. "She probably wasn't ready to pick up the phone if she'd just stormed out on you. Don't blame yourself."

Peter's jaw quivered as if he was about to cry. "Thank you." He stared into Ruth's eyes as if letting go of a part of his guilt—or so she wanted to think. She was just guessing, based on herself and not on Ulrike, whom she didn't even know.

CHAPTER SIXTEEN

2002, SAN FRANCISCO

There was a time in my late forties when I realized that the opportunity to change my life if I ever wanted to had passed me by. And then, in my mid-fifties, I realized that was a good thing.

Ulrike closes William's book and absent-mindedly plays with the pages as she considers his statement. *I'm only thirty-three, but it may be too late to change my life.* She's already done that once, leaving the old gray GDR to land in this bizarre world of grandiose gestures and friendly empty smiles.

Ulrike reclines in her chair in the living room corner Peter lets her use as her office. The wood floor is pleasantly dark, the red curtains bright and meaningful. *At least William seems to understand something.* Late forties! It's unfair—unfair and boring—to have to wait another fifteen years for this ostensible wisdom. *Shouldn't everyone's life be explained to them before they reach that age?* This is what socialism did during her youth: it explained everything and infantilized its victims even after they reached adulthood. They were told what to believe and how to go about believing. They learned that disagreement equaled betrayal.

Ulrike frowns. She is tired of blaming everything on her stupid past. Some people lost their lives to communism. Her own father's time in a Stasi prison made him a different person, extinguished his optimism, and shrank his vigor. *Who am I to complain? I managed to get out early in life.* In the end, communism foamed at the mouth like a rabid dog and perished. Ulrike's escape was easy, compared to many.

Her parents never complain, both excited about a second chance neither had expected. William stopped believing in a second chance well before her parents' age. *Is his sort of despair a privilege? And why am I so impervious to my parents' joy of a second chance? Maybe I was too young when I emigrated.* Questions add up, a ragged pile of uncertainties. Ulrike imagines them metallic, rusty, twisted in a mountain impossible to untangle.

The apartment door clicks, interrupting her thoughts. Peter is back. Ulrike feels a mix of annoyance and relief.

"Good evening." His warm smile.

"How are the windmills and the green grass?"

"The windmills and the green grass are doing great." Peter laughs and sprawls on the couch. "How was your meeting?"

"They rescheduled."

"Rescheduled?" A frown on Peter's face.

"Yes, but I've applied for seven more projects on Craigslist." She forces a smile.

"Great." Peter's tone is indefinite as if he no longer believes in her success in web design. *Quite frankly, he is right as a fucking bullet. Sure, I'll get work eventually, but by then, I will be farther behind. This always happens. Something in me must be resigned to it, but Peter ends up paying a greater share of the bills, more than he can afford.* His credit cards have crossed into five digits, hers maxed out several years back, her credit history a shadow of what it once was.

"Will you need some help this month?" Peter says, as if scripted.

This is not a new conversation.

"I might. Sorry."

"No problem."

Peter's face is still calm, but the smile is no longer sincere—now it's the kind that comes out when he's unhappy but unwilling to fight, still deciding who is right and who is wrong and what's best to do in this carefully considered way of his that sometimes impresses Ulrike and sometimes drives her bananas. *My own fucking fault. I agreed to this arrangement, didn't I?*

"Maybe I should look for a full-time job." Ulrike's offer is half-hearted, her tone as flat as if someone else was using her voice.

"It's a tough market out there. A lot of IT folks lost their jobs a few years ago."

Is Peter trying to discourage her by repeating the excuse she used before, or simply presenting the objective situation as he sees it? They are so tied up in these conversations, neither particularly clear about where their position begins and ends, where the other's point of view applies or doesn't. *This city is too expensive, that's all.*

"I might need to get out of web design altogether."

"That's a thought. What are you interested in doing instead?" Peter's face becomes open and receptive—he's good at that, giving others an opportunity to share their plans.

"I could try to get an adjunct position, but we know how hard it is to get a job with a master's in German history—any history. All the history anyone wants can be looked up online in a matter of minutes. Anyway, a college job might entail moving to some horrible place you have here in this country, a George Bush kind of place." The more Ulrike speaks, the more unpleasant her voice sounds. Her skills are insufficient, but she must earn more than an unskilled worker on minimum wage. A job at McDonald's wouldn't cut it. She's out of options.

"I don't know about moving," Peter says. "I'd miss my job. We would miss my income. You would miss the culture. What about translation or interpreting? You'd be good at it."

He just wants me to fix myself. Ulrike's irritation grows.

"Too many German speakers here in the Bay Area. I'll get lost in the shuffle."

"You might *have to* do something." Peter says, carefully. "This struggle you do is difficult for you and for me. Honestly, I'm getting tired of excuses. I'm also tired of having no money left to speak of. We can't even afford a vacation. Hell, we can't even afford a new couch. I already work overtime."

Ulrike knows she needs to overcome something in herself to change, to break out of this shell of failure. When nothing works, it's tempting to do nothing—but she must develop tools to combat this trend. The state of agreeing in principle but failing to support her agreement in action is intolerable physically: a pressure on her lungs, as if a moment from now, she'll be unable to breathe.

"You can always divorce me, you know." Ulrike regrets and doesn't regret this pronouncement the moment it slides off her lips. "When we met, I told you my situation. Didn't I?" She is just this side of yelling.

"That's your only answer?" Peter's burning eyes are filled with contempt as he stares, his face hard, unsympathetic—a stranger's face. "Come on, Uli, stop being this way. I know I can divorce you; you don't need to tell me that. That's not my intention. But I need you to make an effort if this marriage is going to make any sense. Think of something."

Peter stays calm in situations like this while Ulrike boils. *Asshole.*

"Fuck you!" she yells. "What am I supposed to think of? Fuck!

130

I should have stayed back in Germany. It's all your fault. I would have gone back long ago if I hadn't met you."

There. She's tipped over the edge of the moment, and she knows it.

"Now, that's offensive and unfounded." Peter's face is firm, frozen. "I can't take responsibility for your past choices."

"Well, then go fuck yourself."

Ulrike slaps William's book on the desk and locks herself in the bathroom, and takes her Wellbutrin, her hands shaking as she handles the small plastic bottle. In the mirror, her face is firm and determined. *Still smooth and good-looking, but not warm, like Peter's, even fucking Dietrich's. Definitely not like's Sally's, and most certainly not like Brigita's as I remember her.* In fact, just now, her face looks more rigid and unwelcoming than the faces of everyone she knows.

Ulrike turns the water on and sits on the edge of the tub. *It felt cathartic as ten thousand witches to yell at Peter, but I regret it now.* Her anger is as quick to leave as it is to enter—all that's left is emptiness and puzzlement.

Minutes drift by; hiding in the bathroom becomes ridiculous. Spent and emotionless, Ulrike emerges. Peter is still on the couch—so unlike him, he is always in a hurry to check his email and review his calendar. His face is as grim as a reaper.

"I'm sorry," Ulrike says. "Of course, you can't be responsible for my choices. And I don't regret marrying you. I'm just not sure what to do. But I'll think of something. I'm sorry."

"That's okay." Peter sounds unconvinced, but his face softens a notch or two.

"You know, I've been reading William's book. He doesn't think it's too late to change my life."

"Your life?"

"Anyone our age. He thinks it can be done until you're in your late forties."

"Sounds arbitrary." Peter shrugs. "It's never too late to change your life. Why are you reading that thing anyway? Doesn't it make you more upset?"

From his quick, dry delivery, Ulrike can tell that Peter is still annoyed. No wonder: she herself is annoyed as fuck, but more at herself than anyone else. *Just thinking about life changes is tiresome, let alone implementing them.*

But she must do it, otherwise this not-so-new new life of hers here in the States might explode in her face. There is another way, the William method, but Ulrike is not about to try it—in fact, she is certain she never will. She doesn't believe that everything ought to be solved by a single decision, a grand subtraction.

1986, DRESDEN

Vogel stares into the empty street ahead, asking disconnected questions with long pauses in between. Ulrike is sleepy from the warmth in the car and the superficial questioning. Freezing rain covers the windshield with nasty smears.

She can no longer lie to herself: Vogel will not go away. *He's claimed me as his victim, a de facto collaborator.* The line between a potential rat and a real one is vague and unclear even to the person involved. Anything can be true; anything can be a lie.

Some questions are trivial: about her math grades, whether or not she wants a dog. Amid these, hide the traps. Does her mother go out at odd hours and talk on the phone in foreign languages? Sometimes it's obvious what the safe answer is—other times, less so.

"Can I just come visit you at your office?" Ulrike asks.

She fully expects him to reject the request, to say something offensive. Instead, his comment is neutral and noncommittal. "I'm not always there." His voice trails off as if he regrets every delightful hour he doesn't spend in his gloomy old office.

"I can wait."

"You know how it works. You have to give me something if you want me to do you a favor." He keeps staring straight ahead.

"Something?"

These meaningless stumbling questions slow the conversation. They are broken lenses through which she glimpses their gruesome encounter. *What does Vogel gain? For him, this is just work.* But is a Stasi's work also a passion?

"Information." His voice is neutral. He lights one of his stinky Marlboros, and the smoke fills the car's fake beige space, forcing Ulrike to hold her breath for as long as she can.

It's not long.

"What information?" *It's crystal clear. They want names, obser-*

vations, and personal details that might further enslave my family or some other. "I don't know anything. We've been having these conversations for years." She is nearly yelling.

How has she arrived at this place of being able to express her anger at Vogel? He seems immune to her tone and acts utterly unaffected. *I'm not an object of interest to him, not a human being—I'm a project, a puzzle to crack. He likes puzzles. He would gladly start a new project with any name I might mention.*

"Sometimes asking the same questions is just as good." A small grin cuts Vogel's profile—or it could be something Ulrike imagines there, as in a painting, just the right touch to make the face more sinister. Vogel's face is both sinister and generic.

"Is it? What does it accomplish?"

Vogel turns his head and gives her a surprised, curious look—a moment of humanity in a statue. He quickly turns away. People with empty faces are good actors because they can play any role. Her mother explained that some of the older Stasi were trained under Hitler, but Vogel is middle-aged, perhaps in his fifties, probably too young to have been in the SS.

"How old are you?" she asks.

"How old do I look?"

Should've known getting an answer from him wouldn't be easy. The Stasi ask questions; they don't answer them. A pause follows. She is used to these pauses in their strained conversations.

"Never too young or too old to serve the country," Vogel declares in a flat voice. He doesn't bother to make this preposterous slogan sound sincere.

"Were you in the war?"

His gloved index finger taps on the steering wheel. *Is he nervous? Impatient?* Ulrike has noticed this tick kick in when the conversation becomes uncomfortably personal.

"No, I wasn't. Too young for that. I wish I did, though. My father was killed in Russia."

"You wish you did?" This cuts through to her. She is genuinely surprised. *Like a death wish directed into the past. Like a fuck you to one's own life and to everything the civilization holds dear.*

2002, SAN FRANCISCO

The Tenderloin is a peculiar place to meet a client—her first meeting here. *What the fuck choice do I have, even if the whole deal sounds peculiar?* A telecommunications company offering discount international calling plans. They'd have to be losers to set up an office in this neighborhood, but so is she. In such a need of work, she's willing to do anything. She's a double loser for doing this right before Christmas when most people shop for presents and review travel plans.

Her exchange with Peter is fresh in her mind. She has contacted several translation agencies, checked Craigslist for German-related jobs, and reinforced her commitment to sounding cheerful and positive as fuck in her communications with clients. This last part will take some effort: keeping certain opinions to herself, being a little more diplomatic about design and color preferences, and other admittedly subjective stuff.

Her VW bug is in the garage for repairs: something with the transmission, another expense she can't afford. Today, she's a pedestrian. *Scheisse.*

Ulrike feels confident about the interview. She is smart and well-informed in art and visual design. She is fluent in two languages and has a good command of Italian, which she has studied now and then throughout the last ten years—but these skills are unlikely to help with a website project.

She has a mile to walk. It's a mild day. Ulrike heads down Larkin Street past the boarded-up shop windows. The occasional homeless rest casually on the sidewalk, wrapped in their blankets. *How fucked up that no one can do anything about this. Is Germany like this, too, now? Full of dysfunction, unemployment, hopelessness?*

The street boasts a panorama of casually discarded liquor bottles, paper coffee cups, and disposable food containers with a mush of leftovers inside. Condoms, old socks, unidentifiable scraps of cloth. The smell contributes: a robust mix of urine, vomit, and dust enhanced by burger grease and deep-frying oil emanating from the fast food dives that come and go in this neighborhood.

Ulrike is both disgusted and apprehensive. A woman with a bright red Prada purse on her shoulder is out of place here. How typical of her not to think it through. A homeless man in a padded jacket cartwheels across the street, salutes her. She awkwardly half-salutes back, hoping the guy doesn't think there's more to this exchange. Luckily, he's already walking away, whistling. *Like the happy teapot from that stupid song they sing in this country.* Ulrike is entertained. Still, the tension doesn't leave her.

She has only a block and a half to go when a stinky shadow blocks her path.

Must be out of his mind on drugs. She makes a move to the left, but the ugly bastard moves that way too, blocking her path. *Shit.* The man is tall, broad, twice her weight. He wears a shapeless pair of dirty khaki pants and a bright blue down jacket covered with stains.

"Hey, watch it!" Ulrike moves right.

He moves that way too. *Fuck.* His sunburned face with a contemptuous smile inside a disgusting beard.

"Where're you headed, lady?" The voice is low and hoarse. "This ain't no place for a beautiful lady like yourself. What brings you here if you don't mind me asking? You don't mind, do you?"

'None of your business,' she's tempted to say, but a challenging response may not be the best choice under the circumstances. *How the fuck do I know what's best?* Furtively, she looks around. No one in sight but other shadowy creatures shuffling about or prostrated in secluded corners. *If I scream, no one will hear. Can I run? In these high heels? I can't lose these shoes. Two hundred bucks on sale.*

"I have a meeting." Her voice is small, weak, lost in the unfriendly world.

"A meeting?" The man's tone brims with derision. "No one has meetings in this neighborhood. You turning tricks? Ain't seen you around before."

It takes Ulrike a second or two to understand. She no longer translates everything back into German, but slang still hits her hard. "Tricks? That's crazy. Listen, just leave me alone. I'm not bothering anyone, and I will be late." She presses her purse to her chest. *It would take this hulk of an asshole about half a second to tear it out of my hands.*

The infrequent cars whiz by with motorized indifference.

"Late? I bet your pimp's going to be mad. What do you have in that pretty purse of yours?"

"It's none of your business." She finally says it, but the moment to act in control is lost.

"What if I want to make it my business? What if I'm a man who cares?" He emits a nasty cough of a laugh.

Desperately, Ulrike scans the street.

No rescuers in sight.

"Listen, I'm just going to go." She tries.

"Give me that purse." The man's gigantic hand is on her shoulder, firm. The other dips into his coat pocket and emerges with what is clearly a handle, smooth and black. A cheap kitchen knife. *It looks sharp enough to hurt a human thing.*

CHAPTER SEVENTEEN

1989

"You can track oppression all the way back to Jim Crow if you pay attention," Sarah's animated face was beautiful. "But the Republicans really picked it up with Nixon, with their war on drugs."

Ruth lay stretched on the couch, her back propped against a Tibetan pillow. She loved to hear Sarah talk. Chemistry was all fine and good, but Ruth couldn't stand being ignorant about the injustice that defined American history. The unfairness of what still went on cut through her soul like a poisoned knife. She'd already decided on African American Studies for her minor.

Inspired by Bob Marley's *Rastaman Vibration* on the stereo, Sarah took a massive hit from the pink and blue stained glass bong that sat between them on the coffee table. For their sophomore year, the two girls shared an apartment, a reasonable place in Oakland both sets of parents helped pay for. Just a standard transitory dwelling with gray carpets and beige walls.

"Now they have a couple of new laws to require minimum punishment. One from 1986 and the other from last year. Black folks get arrested disproportionately for petty crimes like minor possession. White people don't get bothered for it. Hell, don't even get me started on all that bullshit." Sarah resumed walking about, gesticulating—her typical mode of existing in the world.

The war on drugs was bullshit, Ruth knew that. But the notion that it affected people of color differently hadn't been as clear to her before, even if she'd developed some idea from endless drug bust stories in the news, most featuring Black faces.

"Tell me more about the war on drugs," Ruth said.

"My uncle is in jail on his second charge. And he wasn't the dealer. He's never done anything harmful in his life."

"Shit." Ruth hadn't expected such a personal story and was honored to hear it. "What happened?"

"He was there during a bust. Had some weed on him."

"Man, that's not fair. What do you..."

The telephone rang on the wall, and Ruth shivered from the unexpected interruption. Sarah picked up the receiver and listened.

"It's for you." She handed it over.

"Hello."

"Ruthie." It was Dad. "I'm sorry to interrupt whatever it is you're doing. It's your mother. She's not well. I had to tell you. You must go and visit her." The information was arriving too quickly; Ruth struggled to keep up.

"Dad, wait. What's wrong with Mom?"

"She'll be okay."

"Great. Now for god's sake tell me what's wrong with her."

"It's embarrassing, but we shouldn't be embarrassed. It's a disease, you see. Turns out your mother has been drinking way more than we had thought." There was a pause. "I had to check her into a rehab."

"What the hell, Dad? How did you let this happen?" Suddenly,

Ruth was mad at her father for the cool façade he directed at her and Mom.

"I'm not your mother's keeper, you know. I have to work. She did her best to hide it, too. It's not that simple."

"I see." Ruth didn't know how to respond, but something in her remained unsettled by her father's attitude.

"She won't have any visitors for a few days, but you should go after that. Write down the address."

"Let me get a pen." Ruth placed the receiver on the couch. "Alcohol," she whispered to Sarah, stretching to get a pen and a notepad from a side table. "Okay, I'm ready."

She wrote it down.

"Would you like to meet for coffee and talk about this face to face?" Dad asked. *How awkward under the circumstances.*

"I think so, Dad. But let me talk to Mom first, okay?"

"Sure, Ruthie. I was hoping you would."

"Bye, Dad. I'll call you soon, okay?"

"Bye."

Ruth hung up, more irritated than concerned for her mother. *What was it that affected me this way? Maybe Dad's rush to enlist me in fixing Mom's problems even though he is more responsible for them.*

"Alcohol?" Sarah asked, deep concern on her face. "Your mom?"

Ruth nodded a few times, still taking in the news.

"Your parents must be quite something." Sarah smiled. "I've never met anyone as perplexed about her parents as you are."

2003

"I was surprised to hear from you." Ruth said.

She sat down, not bothering to order. Saint Frank's was half-empty, familiar. The small white tiles covering the front of the counter were like busy cells linked into a firm structure. Espresso machines whirred like happy atoms. Peter wore a red turtleneck sweater, the color an attractive fit for his well-proportioned face.

"Honestly, at first, I dreaded hearing back from you." Peter hesitated. "I was still angry at you for getting in the middle of the whole thing. Then I realized I may have been unfair. I was unfair. You didn't get in the middle; you just happened to be there. Then I remembered all this other stuff that happened to you. I felt bad. I just wanted to see how you were doing."

"I'm glad you emailed. I'm surprised it's been a month. It feels as if I'm still stuck in the same day." Ruth would have liked to continue complaining, *Problems are growing all around me. It's quicksand, death.* It was too soon to delve into that. "How are you?" she asked.

"A little better. It's been three months since she died, as you know. I'm busy; that helps. I have so much work I don't have time to think about her. And at night, I'm so tired—as if I'm not me. It's like I'm watching my life, and I'm supposed to be sad, but I'm not, or have no energy to be. Do you think it's just an excuse?" He made eye contact, his eyes direct, sincere.

Ruth was surprised at how much he was willing to share, and so easily, as if personal facts were just that—facts.

"No. Not at all. You don't need an excuse."

"What if I didn't love her enough?" He looked at her expectantly again, as if asking Ruth to venture a guess.

"You didn't?" Ruth was unqualified to comment.

She preferred to imagine the life of Peter and Ulrike in a perfect light. *What am I doing here?* It took some effort to remind herself that she'd made a choice to contact this man. As in a chemical reaction, reversal was unavailable. She was going to get through whatever her choices had set into action.

"Ulrike and I...we didn't do all much together. We both were busy all the time. Too busy." Peter sounded apologetic. "I don't know why I'm telling you this, but we are here because of her. The thing is the core structure of my life hasn't changed. Unfair to her, isn't it? She deserves more of a dent in my life." He paused, a pained grimace on his face. "Almost every hour, I'll remember her, and it hurts, really hurts. But what if it doesn't hurt as much as it might someone else? How would I know?"

"We all have our own feelings." Ruth tried to be helpful. "Some react right away, others take longer."

"Yes." Peter seemed to disappear into his thoughts the way he did sometimes.

Ruth was getting self-conscious about the long pause. "I've been meaning to ask you. *Litmanowic.* How did you get that last name?"

"My adoptive parents. My dad's dad was Jewish, a Holocaust survivor."

"I'm glad he made it." A stupid thing to say, but at least it was well-meaning. "For some reason I thought they were Christian. Catholic?"

"Yeah. It's complicated. My grandpa's way of putting a wall between his person and the Holocaust. Grandma was a nurse. They met at the end of the war. It's quite a story." He laughed. "This is San Francisco, the place where everything is mixed up."

"I like that about San Francisco," Ruth said.

"So what did you decide to do about those threats you received?"

"My mom was going to go through Dad's office, but now she seems to think it's best to leave it alone."

"And what do you think?" Peter's eyes on her—interested, calm. *The opposite of pressure.*

"I don't know how to put this behind me if I don't find out. The letter said *don't rock the boat.* I'm not planning to rock it. I just want to sit in it until I know what to do. But I sure wish I could stop thinking about it constantly."

"If you went through your dad's office, you might be able to answer your question, at least for yourself. But what if you don't like the answer?"

"Exactly. I'd be surprised if I liked it. Not much to like about this situation."

Peter smiled pensively. Something about this dilemma was amusing. No denying it: Ruth's life was seeping into Peter's as water penetrates sugar regardless of what sugar might want. *Is that fair to him?*

"I was going to ask you for a picture of Ulrike," she said.

"A picture?"

"Yes. Is that weird?"

"Sure. But I'm getting used to all kinds of weird stuff from you. And I just happen to have a picture in my wallet."

How moving that it would still be there, that a person wouldn't clear out their dead loved ones easily. Ruth had never carried anyone's picture in her wallet.

Ulrike was beautiful and confident, with long blond hair framing her face meaningfully, her penetrating blue eyes firm on Ruth. *Both close and distant, as if you need a special key to get in, but the key will be revealed easily to the right person.*

"It was a tough year for her." Peter's voice entered Ruth's staring contest with the photograph. "One of her clients killed himself a few months ago, right in front of her. The guy wrote this book; Ulrike built a website to promote it. She kept reading it for the last couple of months. I've brought it for you."

"For me? Why? Have you read it?"

"Some of it. I'm too busy these days. Sitting down to read feels like a frivolous gesture. And if I try, I just keep thinking about Ulrike and feel sad and ponder what I could have done differently."

"Thank you, Peter. I'd love to read it."

Peter handed over a cheaply printed book with an airplane on the cover. With a sense of loss, Ruth returned Ulrike's photo.

"Have you ever considered..." she paused, verifying that this inspiration was correct and valuable. "Have you ever considered going there, to visit the place of her accident?"

"Of course. But it seems like a morbid thing to do, doesn't it?"

"Not really. I want to go. Will you come along?"

It took a while for Peter to answer. He looked at his hands. He looked out the window.

"Yes, I will."

CHAPTER EIGHTEEN

2002, SAN FRANCISCO

The attacker's hand on Ulrike's shoulder is huge—the sense of invasion is pungent and disorienting. Vogel's face comes to mind, the face she's been able to forget more and more. Vogel's smirk full of ignorance and contempt, the same smirk President Bush Jr. employs. Anger boils up and overflows. Ulrike grabs the man's hand and rips it off her shoulder. She is not afraid, just annoyed at the prospect of losing her bag in this uneven confrontation.

"Fuck you, asshole." She gives him a vigorous kick on the knee.

The attacker groans in pain. Ulrike is victorious, even excited—but the motherfucker's recovery is unexpectedly fast. He grabs Ulrike's wrist; she can't seem to get it free.

"Not so fast, little lady." His voice a dark growl. Ulrike sets up for another kick when a fist slams into her left eye. The world floats, vague and shaky in color.

When the floating stops, she is on the ground. Her eye hurts. She's disoriented as fuck. The smell of stale beer and dust and cigarette butts assaults her nostrils.

With some effort, Ulrike pushes herself up into a sitting position. Her purse is gone. *Of course.* The attacker is already a couple of blocks away, running toward Market. He turns the corner. Ulrike knows this is the last time she'll see her purse.

She feels indifferent, as if the punch had turned off her emotional responses. She'll have a huge black eye tomorrow. Like an apparition, a police car emerges at the end of the block, rolling in her direction in slow motion. *Fuck! What if they blame me?*

No way. What for?

The cop car pulls over. Ulrike is still sitting on the sidewalk, shaking a little from shock. Vogel's face flickers in her mind, his angry unblinking eyes.

Just as slowly, the car accelerates, drives off, and turns the corner. *They must have assumed I'm just another homeless person.*

Ulrike breathes, relieved.

* * *

Dresden buildings, abandoned just a moment ago, sprout a small army. Each soldier is identical to the rest. Bullets whistle by. One by one, the protesters fall to the ground. Panicked cries fill the air. Stupefied, Ulrike looks around. Dead bodies everywhere. She's the only one standing. All guns are aimed at her.

Ulrike wakes up in sweat, the sheet a trap around her legs. Peter's snoring is helpful at a moment like this, an anchor in her real life. Her eye hurts from the punch.

The dream doesn't visit every night anymore. It arrives several times a year to remind Ulrike that some things are never really finished. That's Sally's interpretation. Ulrike doesn't have a clue what in her life is finished and what is not.

I've never quite woken from this dream, have I? I'm stuck in it.

She is afraid of shots to come. *This is why I'm nowhere in my life. Something inside me hides in a small corner and thinks itself a doomed last protester.*

1986, DRESDEN

Ulrike and Brigita are seventeen. They walk casually, favoring smaller streets. This way, it would be more difficult for a Stasi to follow them and record their conversation. Ulrike's flat must be bugged, considering her father is in prison and she's a person of interest. Brigita, too, by extension. *The Stasi have more high-tech equipment than the KGB and the CIA combined. They show up when no one is home and do their setup.*

Many students continue to avoid Ulrike, which makes her appreciate Brigita all the more.

The two girls are on their way to a meeting. The clandestine opposition group meets at Dresden's old *Kreuzkirche*. The vicars let anyone in; confronting the regime is something most people agree on. The religious façade affords the operation some minimal protection, however flimsy.

"We should write to the Western newspapers," Brigita says.

Initiatives are in the air, the city overflows with them.

"Yes, but how? And say what? It would have to be something they don't know yet. Besides, the letter would never get through the mail." Ulrike's reaction to her friend's naïve optimism alternates between gratitude and irritation. *Enthusiasm is a good, but doesn't she know how things work?* "The West can't meddle in this country's laws. I wish they could."

They pass the newly reconstructed *Semperoper* Opera House, its cheerful triangle insisting that art and symmetry will prevail. Opened in 1841 and destroyed by fire in 1869, it was rebuilt and then destroyed in the Allied bombing of February 13, 1945. Forty years later, it was rebuilt again, on the cheap, to look the same as its predecessor. This third incarnation opened last February.

The building means more than Ulrike can explain, both good and bad. Some say it's wired to record every conversation. Some say it's the symbol of Dresden. Some call it an empty talisman of a dying empire, a shadow of a shadow of a former building. *Some say the Nazis gave birth to the Stasi, and Dresden will never be pure again. Nazi, Stasi—even the two words are nearly identical.*

"Your family's story is special," Brigita says. "Your father helped people to freedom and paid the price for that. It's a great story. We must be able to get it out."

"Our family is no different than hundreds, thousands of other people. What can anyone do?" *I might grow old staring at pictures of Lenin and Honecker.*

"Let me make sure I understand correctly." Brigita is determined the way she gets, one of her qualities Ulrike loves and hates. "Are you saying there's nothing to be done? The situation can't be helped? We should just give up and do nothing?"

"No. No, that can't be true, can it? But it feels that way sometimes, doesn't it? Remember 1984?"

Ulrike's parents used to hide a copy of Orwell's novel, a West German printing, behind other books on the top shelf. Barbara handed it to Ulrike in 1984, a sinister touch. Ulrike insisted she must share the novel with her friend. The rule was simple: the book was to be read only at the Schumacher flat. Taking it out would be too risky. When things heated up with the Stasi, even owning a copy became too dangerous. Barbara gave it away.

Soon, Kreuzkirche stands before them with its narrow windows and towers. Under the high domes, the group discusses sabotage techniques in the workplace, information dissemination initiatives, and other activities intended to undermine the regime. They've achieved little yet—it's not obvious how to get started.

Ulrike keeps the group from her mother. *In this country, the less one knows about one's loved ones, the less risky for all involved.* She's become good at hating her country since meeting Vogel three years ago, and especially since her father's arrest.

2002, SAN FRANCISCO

"Hi *Mama*," Ulrike says into her red telephone.

She is home, taking a break from the incredibly annoying hours of looking for work online. Even in January, the apartment is filled with generous afternoon light, insisting that things aren't as crappy as they appear to be. The blue walls are just a little bluer than the sky outside.

"Hello, dear." Barbara sounds distant.

"Where are you? I've been thinking of you today."

"Right here in the city." Her mother laughs. "And you?"

"I was thinking about Papa's years in prison."

"Oh, darling. That was a terrible time." Ulrike can hear that her mother still feels the horror of those days.

"It was, wasn't it? Anyway, you're not traveling? I'm surprised."

"Well..." Barbara paused. "I'm going to Rome next Monday for a conference. Are you okay, dear?"

"Do you wonder sometimes if your life is broken in advance just because of the kind of past we've had?" Ulrike is on the verge of tears, but she's unsure why.

"I don't think my life is broken, Uli. And neither is yours. That we grew up in shit doesn't mean we have to feel guilty about it. I don't see anything broken about your life. You might have to up your anti-depressants. Big deal! Be contemporary about this. Didn't Sally say so? Remember how I was back in the late 80s? Checked out on hopelessness. It runs in the family, dear. No need trying to fight it."

"I'm not trying to fight it, Mother."

Ulrike is about to mention the mugging but thinks better of it. That's not something Barbara can help with—just a random fact of city life. *I'm alive—that's what matters.*

"How are you dealing with that client's suicide? Such a horrible thing to do."

"Oh, I don't know." Ulrike gathers her thoughts. "I'm okay, but I still think about it a lot. Sally and I are working on it."

"Good. And how's Peter?"

"Oh, Peter! Peter's okay. Peter's fine, just fine."

"Don't underestimate your husband, darling." Barbara is good at reading Ulrike's tone.

"I don't. It's not his fault, I know."

"You two will be fine. And if not, it's okay to try again with another person. I was so scared when your father asked for a divorce. But afterward, it made perfect sense. Now that I'm with Jack, I see how wrong your father and I were for each other, even if it took us centuries to understand that. I don't mean to criticize him, dear. Especially after everything that happened to us. To him. And you—look at yourself. You're young, beautiful, smart."

"Not so young anymore."

"Don't make me laugh." Her mother laughs anyway. "I like Peter. Peter's a good man. I'm not trying to put any ideas into your head. Just reminding you that anything's possible. Nowadays, there's room for more than one life in each of our lives."

Is that true?

There's barely room enough for a single life, in me.

CHAPTER NINETEEN

2003

The lab was empty, the silence augmented only by the hum of the fridges and the freezers, which Ruth no longer noticed. She felt like a child amid all this silence. She'd read something similar in that book by Ulrike's client, his recollections of entering the workspace before others, enjoying silence where silence was rare. Apparently, some of his best ideas came to him during these brief morning minutes with a cup of coffee. *How terrible it must have felt for Ulrike to witness the guy's suicide. What an ugly thing to do.*

Ruth took a sip of coffee and held it in her mouth, letting the bitterness sink in. She added a few supplementary spoons when she was the one to start the coffee machine. Extra caffeine molecules had never hurt anyone. *Coffee is supposed to be coffee, not decaf (an absurd notion), nor water with a barely noticeable trace of brown.*

Is taking Peter to the scene of the accident really a good idea?

She'd offered; it was too late to retract. Ruth needed to see that place again. She'd been avoiding it. She'd been avoiding everything.

What about my dissertation? Since her father's death, she'd barely written a page. She struggled with the daily maintenance of life. *I better snap out of this stupor, or I'll never get the stupid PhD.*

Ruth's lab bench was the opposite of neat. Gloves, glassware, colorful Time Tape, and paperwork contested for space, with her dirty lab coat carelessly resting over the whole mess. *How can I ever care for a partner, a husband, or another human being if I can't keep my bench organized?*

She took a sip from her plastic bottle. The material cracked in her hand, incongruously loud. Dad had always teased her about her plastic bottles and her propensity to take H_2O supplies on the road. Plastic, chemistry's best invention. Polymers, our fragile DNA itself a touching example. The good old Belgian, Leo Baekeland was already a millionaire from his work on film technologies when he created Bakelite, the first plastic. *How sad that he became a recluse in his old years. But no one cares about old years. No one cares about anything. Anything outside their own needs, goals, secrets.* Ruth's thoughts were drifting. It would be a slog of a day, but she looked forward to seeing Peter.

* * *

This used to be Ruth's place to relax. The ocean, the beach, Cliff House. Other people relaxed in other ways. They walked their dogs, sang karaoke, had sex. Ruth used to come here to observe the motion.

Just three blocks from her home on Fulton, the hill gradually rose at its southern end, a web of paths crisscrossing the small wild area. It grew to a forty-foot bluff presiding over Cliff House.

Ruth was captivated by the two streams of cars and the ocean's mass in the background, indifferent, dismissive of all human effort. For a moment, she'd forgotten about Peter, who followed her, slightly out of breath.

Ruth turned her head. In his green sports jacket, Peter was overdressed for this small hike. Still, he looked great in this outfit, just as he would in any other.

The grass was springy under her feet. It wasn't a long path. Soon, they reached the spot. The curving highway below, the running vehicles.

"This is it," Ruth said.

"She was going this way, wasn't she?" Peter pointed to the right toward Cliff House.

"Yes."

The silence lasted forever, pushing at Ruth's edges of comfort. For a moment, she regretted bringing Peter here. *Will this scene become a setting for his nightmares?* It all came back: the white car, the truck, the giant tomato, the smoke, the driver's hesitant approach. *Something about the accident still eludes me. What is it?*

"It's not the worst way to go," Peter said. "A beautiful place."

The sun was preparing to retire. Red edges grew around everything in sight. The white car just down the road could be Ulrike's. *Is it? Wait.* Ruth was disoriented. The car remained intact as it disappeared from sight.

"Sometimes I didn't know if I loved her at all." Peter stood facing the ocean.

"Maybe this is how love always is? It's hard for me to say."

Ruth's brief list of unsatisfactory relationships flashed through her mind. She wouldn't call any of them love.

"What if it was about convenience more than love?" Peter's hand cradled his face. "Trouble is, I can't go back and measure my feelings. I just don't know. I wish I did. I wish I did." His face crumples. "Thank you for bringing me here."

1989

Ruth's comfortable chair gently supported her as she sat by her mother's bedside in what would have resembled a well-appointed hotel room if not for her mother's green face and the fact that medical personnel remained just outside 24-7.

"How do you feel, Mother?"

As usual, Linda took her time to respond.

"Shitty, dear. Really shitty. Oh, I wish I could have a drink," she said theatrically.

"Do they feed you well?"

"I don't know, darling. They offer all these dishes I love, but all I want to do is throw up."

"You'll feel better soon."

Ruth wasn't sure her reply had conveyed enough optimism. *Is that even accurate?* Questions rushed through Ruth's head. *What happened? How did she let it get to this?* It was pointless to ask. Her mother had neither the skill nor the desire for self-scrutiny.

How did Dad ever marry this woman? Ruth laughed briefly, struck by the question's simple and necessary cruelty.

"What's so funny?"

"Nothing." Ruth made a muscular effort to remove the smile from her face. "How long do you have to stay here?"

"Oh, I don't know. A couple of weeks." Her mother sighed. "It's not too bad, actually. At least I don't have to deal with your father and all his secrets."

"I know, Mother, I know." *How did she ever marry that man?* "Why do you stay with him?" Ruth petted her mother's sweaty arm, imagining a C_2H_5OH ethanol molecule Linda was so in love with.

"For the longest time, I stayed for you."

"For me?" Ruth scoffed.

The way her mother had conducted her life, cranky and

distracted, rotating entirely around her axis, Ruth couldn't accept this as a gift or an objective reality.

"Spare me your skepticism, Ruthie." With shaking hands, Linda grabbed the half-filled plastic water glass from the bedside table and took a few urgent gulps. "At least you're safe and healthy and have good values. And now you're getting a good education too."

This much sounds correct.

"What about now?" Ruth asked. "Why not leave him now that I'm out of the house?"

Linda seemed to consider this for a few seconds. "I guess, at some point, I just ran out of energy."

Such a vulnerable disclosure was unusual for her mother. They both remained silent for a while. Ruth was unsure what to say.

Marie Curie wasn't known for an interest in alcohol. She'd had stronger elements to play with. And Ruth, too, saw little point in drinking, despite the freedom and the parties college life brought along. *How did Mother develop this drive? Is it true that the whole thing is about Dad and his secrets?*

It was difficult to worry about Linda, who had abdicated any worry for her for as long as Ruth could remember. *This drinking problem—isn't it just another way to spit in everyone's face, to grab everyone's attention? A giant fuck you to the family and the world.*

What about me?

What part of her was simply borrowed from her parents? She was too secretive, bad at making connections. *I still have so much to learn about myself.* What a luxury, these several years of school between her and the adult life full of choices and responsibilities. The space between her and her parents was itself a luxury.

Poor Mother. What is it she's missed out on? What chemical components are responsible for ambition, for craving meaning in one's life?

CHAPTER TWENTY

2002, SAN FRANCISCO

Ulrike is home on this gray day. *I spend too much time at home, especially for a person prone to depression. A full-time job could do me good.* But those are even harder to find than individual web design projects. *It's a fuckety-fuck world.*

Brigita's email on the screen before her makes her nostalgic for her distant friend,

> Uli, you should drop everything and move here. And bring that cute husband of yours. But you better watch it because all the girls here will hit on him. Seriously, though: it's the best time to buy in East Berlin. A hundred thousand of your silly green dollars will get you a good three-room flat the size of yours and in a beautiful neighborhood. You can buy, rent, or do whatever you want, but buying makes way more sense since prices will DEFINITELY go up. I can guarantee that. You can do your web design, and Peter can do any number of things. I know, it's going to be a transition

for him, but at least promise me you'll think about it. Promise? It's the most liberal place in the world, the best place for an individual—if you know what I mean. You haven't been here since before the Ice Age, so you have no clue. Consider it!

The email continues, but Ulrike is reluctant to read it all at once. Her friend doesn't write often. *How interesting about Berlin. The world evening things out, healing the wound the former GDR had opened on the skin of Europe.* Berlin holds way more attraction than Ulrike's hometown. *Dresden, the asshole of Germany.* The place still doesn't want to acknowledge any responsibility; it rebuilds the façade without rebuilding the soul. Ulrike doesn't like to go back. She's visited only twice since she left in 1991. She fears the Stasi lurking about, hiding behind their aged faces.

When she lived there, the Russians pulled all the strings. Putin's black Volga must have passed her by on Dresden streets. He served as the local KGB chief between 1985 and 1990. *It may have been a European car, not a Volga at all. Those fucking Russians always preaching new world order while using Western goods.*

What an idea, to return to Germany. After last week's mugging, she knows San Francisco is not always a friendly place—but neither is any city. *To give up this emigration project, to leave this land of freedom clowns? And go back to my own formerly fucked up and now prospering stupid Mutterland?* In some ways, it makes sense. But it's the last thing Ulrike would ever do.

Despite their occasional superficiality, Americans are a cheerful and friendly nation. She loves living among them. She remembers the unsmiling GDR, the average gloomy, closed-off face a perfect match for a world where information was a weakness and a weapon in the wrong hands and no one knew which hands were wrong. *No, thank you.*

Peter would never agree to move. He loves his job like a puppy loves a bone, and it's a good job, not meaningless nonsense like some of Ulrike's web design projects.

What would she do back in Germany? Something else would fall into her hands—something her friends and former classmates might offer, or just a thought that might come to her once she is back in the world of her first language.

But she prefers English. *The positive language.* It provides so much more comfort and intimacy. There are things she can discuss in English she'd be embarrassed to mention in her native tongue. Personal, emotional things. German has bad connotations in Ulrike's life, and much worse in the lives of so many people everywhere.

In films, one returns to one's home country after years and years and finds everyone interested, engaging, invested, willing to meet, to help. *My return won't make for a good film. Apart from Brigita, no one would care.* Ulrike walks into the bathroom, and a brief stab of pain vibrates through the left side of her face. Involuntarily, her hand covers it. The pain is gone soon, replaced by the vague discomfort she's recently felt around her bruise.

She flushes and walks over to the mirror. Some of the new wrinkles she'd hoped to lose are still there. *Aging is not so bad.* Despite the bruise on her face, she might be in the best shape in her life. Her face is slimmer than in her twenties.

Her eyes are sadder.

That's self-projection if such a thing exists. She smiles to herself and is satisfied with her smile and with what American dentistry has done to her teeth.

A more precise question is: what does she *want* to do with her life? If financial pressures were removed, what would she become? *Fucked if I know. Isn't this sad, to be thirty-three and so unsure about what I might do if I weren't continuously pushed around by circumstances?*

The evening is settling in with its bright sky colors.

"Sorry I'm late." Peter's voice.

He is awfully charming today, his smile friendly and genuine. *Not the perfunctory lip curve he deploys when he's preoccupied with his office affairs and saving the environment's ass.*

"That's okay." She smiles too. "I assumed you might be. Hey, I got a down payment to cover my share of the rent." It feels good to say this. *For once, I'm not the monumental fuck-up I tend to be.*

"That's great." Peter's face lights up. "I'm so glad. It helps a lot."

"How's my eye?" Ulrike laughs.

"Your eye is beautiful, just beautiful. I've never seen such an attractive shade of yellow or such an elegant inflammation."

"Thank you, sir."

Peter takes her into his huge hug, and Ulrike is lost in his body. Now she remembers why she loves this man—his smile, his embrace. She is grateful for him, for this life, crazy but different, so much more meaningful than her Stasi-controlled childhood.

She is aroused, and her lips search, find Peter's lips. He drops his briefcase. Her hands on his shirt, pulling it off. *By god's ass, this man is attractive without a shirt, if only I can undo my belt fast enough.*

1986, DRESDEN

The kitchen is submerged in low tones of a dying evening as Ulrike sits at the kitchen table, checking her homework.

"They called again," Barbara says without turning around. She is puttering with something in the sink.

"Yeah?" Ulrike is unconcerned. "The Stasi do that kind of thing. Call you and hang up. Why worry, at this point? Besides, we shouldn't be discussing these things here, *Mutter*. Surely our place is bugged. Why do you worry so much?"

Every feature of Barbara's shadowed face reveals the exhaustion from this new life as a wife of an enemy of the state. She stops fussing with the dishes and sits at the table across from Ulrike. "Why do I worry? Oh, well. Complaining won't make it better."

"I miss dad too." Ulrike sighs. "I know it's not the same."

"Wait." Barbara walks over to the bright blue portable *disco* record player with its minimalist design and its two knobs. She picks a random LP from a stack next to the player. The second knob is turned all the way to the right. Bach's inventions fill the air.

Ulrike has just turned seventeen. She's been dealing with the Stasi for a long time, but she still feels too young for this—as if, in some way, the time to assume full responsibility for herself is still ahead. *What a royally screwed up world to spend my formative years in—and probably all of my life.*

"There's talk about the Solidarity in Poland and what protesters might be able to do here, at home," Barbara says. "Have you heard?"

"Yes, Mutti. Poland is wild and free, but here in the ass-brained GDR, every one out of ten is a spy. We have better organized oppression." Her country, a deadly snake with a nice red bow, a red flag and a smile.

"And Gorbachev?" Barbara asks.

"Yes. Gorbachev. It's hopeful. We'll have to see."

"I've never told you this..." Barbara begins—then she is stuck. Her eyes are elsewhere.

"What?"

"I wasn't sure if I should share it with you. You know how it is with some things. You don't want people around you to know. Not because you don't trust them, but because you don't want to burden them with protecting it."

"Protect what? What are you talking about?"

"Well..." Barbara folds her arms on her chest, her face a series of hesitant expressions. "Well, I helped your dad with some of the smuggling. I didn't do much, but I helped copy some handouts and write some text. This and that and other things. It wasn't much. I wasn't the one planning it or anything, but still, I was part of it. And, you see, I just thought it was the honest thing to tell you now. I don't know why the Stasi didn't arrest me. I really don't. They probably don't have the evidence. Your dad didn't turn me in. Don't forget this, Uli. No matter what, he didn't turn me in. I had to tell you, you see?"

CHAPTER TWENTY-ONE

2003

The chilly evening hung heavily with its gray sky and unpredictable wind gusts. Peter's office on Market Street wasn't far from Ruth's. He'd agreed to meet after work to help her go through her father's things at the Russian Hill house. After their trip to the accident site, they'd spoken on the phone two or three times, their conversations short and friendly. A concern for each other was developing, almost a kind of friendship—at least, this is how Ruth described it to herself. She hoped she wasn't exaggerating.

Ruth got there first. The Bay Bridge lay in the distance, a forgotten crown. The meeting place, her old playground at Sue Bierman Park, sat across from the pier, skyscrapers looming over it. Ruth was reminded of 9-11, when the notion of skyscraper had been redefined. *Wasn't there a small building right around here with the words Trade Center or something similar?* Still, this atrocity dominated the news, now building up to a war someone must find enough common sense to prevent.

What does Sarah think about all this? It was tempting to email or call, but their friendship had cooled since Sarah's move. *It must be my fault, somehow.* She could still hear Sarah's voice in her head. 'The fucking W. Bush, a perfect Republican, a latent racist and an imbecile. Don't even get me started on Dick the Dick Cheney, Nixon's evil heir.'

The world weighed on Ruth as these skyscrapers weighed down on the landscape. Suddenly, she was uneasy about going through her father's office without securing her mother's consent.

Wait. I can't know in advance what stage of inebriation Mom might be in. It was safer and more efficient just to show up. The notion of exposing Peter to her boozing monster of a mother was terrifyingly awkward. Ruth regretted inviting him. *Why do I always make the most unfortunate of social moves? Too late to change my mind—that would be most inconsiderate and inconsistent.*

A mother with a child on either side walked briskly by; then Ruth was alone again. *If such a thing is possible while a hundred thousand office workers breathe within a mile's radius.* Ruth was familiar with this particular solitude of cities, the easy lostness amidst the indifferent multitudes. *The gray clouds are snails chasing one another out of the visible sky.* Ruth watched them for a while and began to relax. Then Peter was there.

"You're early." Ruth wasn't sure if that was true.

"I'm sorry." Peter's charming smile was at the ready, as usual. *Those dimples.*

"No, no, that's great. It's good to see you."

"Shall we go?"

For some reason, Ruth wasn't prepared for such an immediate departure. She'd expected Peter to sit down.

"Sure. We can take the No 5 bus. It's just a few blocks that way." She pointed.

"I can drive." Peter's brows went up in a geeky and charming way.

His Volvo was parked nearby. The car brought Ruth's thoughts

165

back to Ulrike. *How many times has Ulrike ridden in this passenger seat? Was she a good driver? What was her chemical formula? What made her tick?*

"You said you had a fight?" Ruth asked.

"Who did?" Peter's face was so compelling as he focused on the traffic ahead.

"You and Ulrike, the day she died."

"Oh."

The pause was long enough to consider whether her question had been appropriate. So many of her questions ended up in poor timing.

"Did I mention that?" Peter asked. "Yes, yes, that's one of the things that drove me crazy. We often had fights. That was nothing out of the ordinary." He paused. "You know, somehow, I don't think about it as much anymore. I mean, the particulars of that day. It's easy to go down that road." Peter looked left and right, preparing to make a turn, and waited for a car that blew around the corner without a signal. "Easy to get stuck wondering what would have happened if we hadn't had that fight, if I hadn't let her run off that day, if we hadn't met at all. But you can't do that; you just can't. It wasn't even a fight, really." Peter closed his eyes for a moment. "I can't blame myself just because I was part of her life and didn't arrange that particular day differently."

Clearly, these things have been brewing in his head. He was animated, his brown eyes full of energy.

"You're right," Ruth said. "You can't blame yourself. No one can account for every repercussion of each move. It's not a lab experiment."

Peter threw her a quick sideways glance. "A lab experiment?"

"Did I mention I was a chemist?"

"Oh, that's right. You did."

The streets were busy, cars abandoning downtown like lines of ants escaping fire. For a while, they didn't talk.

"What do you hope to find in your dad's office?" Peter briefly turned his head to meet her eyes.

"I don't know. The cops have already been through all his stuff. The whole idea is ludicrous, really—I'm so sorry. I just wanted to take a look around and think about how I might act if I had a secret. But that's ludicrous, too, even more so. I've never been good at keeping secrets. No point to them, as far as I'm concerned. Maybe I can guess his hiding place."

"Nothing wrong with trying." *How did he develop that skill of reassurance?* Peter took a right on Van Ness, confident behind the wheel.

Parking took an interminable emptiness of time, perhaps fifteen minutes, as they circled the narrow streets awash with people, busy like molecules, and ended up three blocks away. They didn't talk much as they walked. And then, here they were, at her parents' door, blue and old-looking, hiding a world that had nearly fallen apart in a matter of months.

Instantly, Ruth was filled with panic.

As she pressed the door button, doubt overwhelmed her again. She listened desperately for any reaction inside.

None followed.

Ruth felt relieved.

She pressed the button once more, already digging in her purse for her key. *It would be most convenient if Mother were out.* Peter stood by, neutral and seemingly unperturbed.

Then she heard a faint sound from within.

Ruth waited.

Her mother's shuffling steps, approaching.

After some delay, the door opened. Linda's face was pale, unkempt. She kept blinking as if her fragile eyes could not tolerate the light.

"Ruthie?"

"Hi, Mom. This is Peter. I've mentioned him."

"Peter? Yes, yes, Peter. Yes! Now I recall." *Right. Surely, she doesn't remember the small bits I've shared concerning Peter.* "I'm Linda. Nice to meet you, young man."

"Hi, Linda. It's very nice to meet you too." Peter extended his hand; they shook.

"To what do I owe this pleasure? You two, you look determined." Linda glanced from one of them to another and back a few times as if working on a puzzle. "What's on your mind? But first things first. Won't you please come in?"

They followed Linda to the living room.

"Can I offer you two a drink?"

"Sure, a drink would be nice." Peter was clueless.

"Great." Linda's smile shined. "I was just going to make one. I'll make a drink for all of us and then we'll sit down and talk."

"Thank you, Linda," Peter said. "It's very kind of you."

The house was so painfully familiar, still *home* to Ruth.

"He's *very* polite, isn't he?" Linda commented as if Peter had stepped out of the moment. He didn't seem annoyed, his reaction constrained to a small smile.

"Sorry," Ruth whispered upward, toward Peter's ear.

"No worries," he whispered back.

They accompanied Linda to the adjacent kitchen, where a large half-empty vodka bottle reigned on the green marble counter. The place was in better order than Ruth had feared: only a few dirty dishes in the sink. Her mother was probably not eating much, deriving most of her calories from liquids.

The ceiling light was off. A series of small flood lights illumined the tall space, creating many busy shadows in and around the two arced entrances. *These shadows must be great fun when you're drunk.* Suddenly, Ruth felt cynical and ungenerous toward her mother and the entire world. The stress of the last few months was taking its toll.

"Will vodka and cranberry do for you?" Linda was all smiles.

"I'm afraid I've run out of most other options. Wait, I have some red wine."

"Vodka and cranberry is just fine." Peter gave Ruth an inquisitive glance.

"Yes, mother, that's great. Listen, I'm not going to beat around the bush. We're here to take a look at Dad's stuff. I tried to call you, but you didn't pick up." *Why did I have to add this last part, a complete fabrication? Am I getting manipulative in response to Mom's tactics?* "I'm just going to look, that's all." Ruth raised her palms in the air before her like miniature shields, as if something as feeble as these small hands could preempt her mother's resistance.

"Didn't we talk about this, dear? We should leave that stuff alone. What are you hoping to find? We'd be much better off just moving on with our lives." Her mother didn't appear annoyed, just puzzled by Ruth's intention.

So this is her way of moving on. Getting drunk by late afternoon. Maybe this was right for her mother? She seemed more at ease than Ruth.

"I don't know," Ruth said. "I don't know. I just wanted a few minutes to take a look around. I might see something others didn't. I can barely breathe with all these uncertainties."

"I thought you two were here to let me know you were getting married."

A non sequitur if I've ever heard one. Ruth felt her face going red. Peter remained comfortable, relaxed, immune to small embarrassments. He had "people skills." As if to confirm, he sent Ruth a charming smile.

"I'm afraid not, mother," Ruth said.

"Linda, I'm so sorry about your husband's death." Peter's voice was soft, genuine. "Ruth told me. It's terrible."

"Thank you kindly, Peter. It was an awful thing. And I'm so sorry about your wife."

So she does remember who Peter is. Ruth was shocked. *I should have given her a little more credit.*

"All this death," Linda continued. "Why don't we all just have drinks and talk and forget this nasty business?" She swiftly deposited ice cubes into each of the three tall blue glasses she must have fetched while Ruth wasn't looking. Linda's hands trembled as she served the drinks. "That old fool, I don't know what nonsense he got himself into. Clearly, it was over his head. And now you want to drag yourself into it, along with your mother and this nice young man? Come on, Ruthie." The last bit was more a plea than a demand.

"I just want to look, mother. I have to. Relax. I'm not committing to any course of action until we've talked about it."

"You're just as stubborn as your father." Linda's voice rang sharp.

Ruth did her best not to take offense. It was Peter who reacted unexpectedly, his face splitting into a huge grin.

"This is what *my* mother keeps saying to me."

"Let's drink to that." Linda raised her glass.

An unconvincing toast, but they all clinked and drank.

"Would you like to sit down in the living room?" Linda asked as if reading Ruth's thoughts.

Peter's inquisitive eyes sought out Ruth's.

"No, mother. We need to do this before we get drunk. We'll chat later, how about that?"

"This tastes nice—thank you," Peter said gallantly. His long fingers looked elegant holding the glass. The glass looked elegant in his hand. Linda was skilled at selecting the best in everything.

But Peter—how charming this man was. *Ulrike's—what?—ex-husband? Or ex-Ulrike's husband? There's a word for it. What is it now?*

Widower.

Something else teetered on the edge of her mind. What was it?

Something related to Ulrike's client who'd committed suicide? The world was teeming with connections, a collision of spider webs.

"Do whatever you like, Ruthie." In one gulp, Linda finished her beverage. "Go ahead, you two. I'm just going to refill my drink."

Ruth led the way up the narrow blue stairs. The second floor was warmer in the evening. The vacuum cleaner rested in the middle of the landing, triumphant, its long cord still plugged in. *How impressive that Mother still makes such small efforts.* Ruth turned to her right and walked down the hall, Peter following. The door of her father's office was closed as if he were inside, working, as on all those childhood nights. *What what is he labored on behind closed doors, between all his so-called business travels?*

She breathed in and pulled. The door creaked, and an image flashed in Ruth's mind: playing hide and seek with friends during a sleepover. She'd been eight or so. She remembered only some moments from that day, but apparently, the game took over the entire house. Out of breath and panting like a dog, Ruth pushed open a door and entered. Her dad's right hand moved as if to lock something in the desk's drawer. Ruth was surprised and embarrassed to see him, to realize it was his room she had invaded.

"I'm sorry, Daddy," she had said.

"That's okay, Ruthie. Now, go play. And please knock next time. Barging in is impolite."

That was it, a mild reprimand, but the awkwardness of her misstep had stuck with her—and his secretive move. Ever since, her subconscious must have been working on this problem: her father hiding something.

The air in the office was stale. A thin layer of dust had settled. The window shades were drawn, making Ruth claustrophobic. She walked over and drew the curtains apart, tilted the window open. Her dad's massive oak desk with its old-fashioned lamp dominated the room. A pile of papers remained unprocessed. The room felt very different without her father in it.

It was good to have Peter nearby. Her mother, not so much. Ruth wasn't sure if, at any point in her life, Mother had been on her side. Typically, Linda was merely a parallel traveler driven by her own agenda.

Linda came upstairs to join them and plopped into one of the chairs positioned opposite the desk, nearly splashing her drink during this maneuver. Ruth walked around the desk and sat in her dad's chair. Peter hung by the door, apparently uncertain where to position himself. Immediately, he addressed Linda with polite questions.

Ruth's thoughts refused to stay with the inane chat. She imagined how her father might have felt sitting here. A difficult exercise since he'd been a tall, muscular man, and she a small woman. She began by running her palm over the desk's bottom surface. Bad idea borrowed from so many movies—her finger shot a signal of pain. A splinter.

Ruth was able to extract it without tweezers while Peter and her mother remained deep in conversation. Their statements didn't make it through to Ruth as cohesive speech, just a river of language in which only the occasional word stood apart, a rare agent in a complex chemical solution.

She knelt beside the chair, the desk obscuring her view of the other two. Now she could focus better. But on what? She looked and looked, her eyes blurry from examining each square inch. Just a regular desk, with its perfectly boring bottom and the two sides of solid wood. All surfaces were even, revealed no hidden compartments.

"What was his name?" Peter asked Linda.

Whose name? Ruth tuned them out again.

Why assume the hiding place was here? If she had to hide something, her own desk would be the most unlikely place. The place everyone would search. Or the place no one would bother with, assuming a sane person doesn't hide things in an office desk?

Ruth was out of her element on the topic of reliable hiding places. She didn't even know what she was looking for.

Think, brain, think. It must be somewhere else in this room. She remembered that Coppola movie, *The Conversation*, whose character tears his house apart in search of a surveillance bug. Books and movies were Ruth's only windows onto the world of hidden agendas and secret identities. Something at her core was still offended by the fact that her life became infected with that stuff. *No one asked me—and now I'll never be free of it.*

Ruth sighed. She wished for silence. She wished for a cup of coffee instead of this drink that hovered on the edge of the desk. *Mother's little spy.*

CHAPTER TWENTY-TWO

All the lights were on when I got home, even the Christmas lights outside. It was May. She'd gone through the trouble of threading the cord through the window to light them up. The music was on, traditional carols. My mother always hated that type of music.

I called out—no response. I remember that moment very well. As if I knew something and didn't know it at the same time. I didn't have the words for it then. Not sure if I do now. When I saw her, I wasn't surprised.

She was wearing her favorite dress, the one Dad had given her on their tenth anniversary. It was red, provocative with its brightness and its simple, revealing cut. I was eleven, old enough to feel it and remember it, to give it words later. She had stayed in shape; the dress looked great on her. She wore

174

red leather gloves. Can you imagine that? Red leather gloves.

I wonder if she chose the red gloves to match the blood. Or the dress? She was always the one to care for detail: the look of things, the shapes, the colors. I inherit this from her.

She didn't leave a note. She'd cut her throat with the same long kitchen knife she'd used the night before to slice a tomato. I haven't been able to enjoy tomatoes ever since. The knife was dull. It must have taken the right angle and lots of determination to keep pushing the blade through even as life was leaving her body. This is my nightmare— being there in the moment of her self-extermination. Trying to stop it, but always, always failing.

With a loud slap, Ulrike shuts William's book. *What the fuck! What the fucking fuck!* This bit on page 213 reads as if written just for her to explain William's red blood in a black-and-white setting. *So he'd planned it all along? He must have assumed that I'd read his book. That I would immediately understand his performance.*

Had he planned it? That's precisely the question she's been unable to get out of her head. For some reason, she feels she must know, even as she acknowledges the fuck out of the fact that she can't really know. *The act was so gruesome and so violent only a complete asshole would have planned such a performance for another unfortunate homo sapience.*

Ulrike is in bed, delaying the moment when she must jump up and get busy. More than anything, she is furious at William for this surrender, for repeating his mother's act. *Sad and unoriginal.*

Immediately, she is ashamed of thinking about it in such terms. *Unoriginal?* William must have made his decision for different reasons, succumbing to inescapable pressures of his own, inside or outside his own mind, his book, his ridiculous website, the East German web designer showing up in the middle of an existential tragedy. She feels bad for arriving just then. William may have been still alive. Sure, Sally keeps assuring her that his act was not Ulrike's responsibility, but it's easier to say than to believe.

And then, like a lightbulb flipped on in her brain, she can see the difference. *What William's mother did was innocent in its own completeness—she was already dead by the time she was discovered. William upped the ante by enlisting me as a witness.* "This is my nightmare—being there, in the moment of her self-extermination."

1987, DRESDEN

When the doorbell rings, Ulrike is cleaning. She is sprawled on the floor, trying to sweep the barely accessible area under the bathtub where dust goes to sleep. Her mother is still at work. She sighs and scrambles to get up. *In this life, this country, a visit is not always good news.*

She is eighteen and just back from vocational school, where she is training to be a typist. With her Stasi problem, University is not for her. *I'm lucky to have settled on a practical skill.* They are being trained on old, repaired machines. Computers are coming at some point. *As long as the keys don't stick.*

"Who is it?" Ulrike asks through the door.

"Uli? It's me, Papa."

The voice—his voice!

Ulrike's hands shake as she struggles to unlock the door. Something in her mind lags behind as if expecting a provocation—something else hopes, believes. One more try, another—the lock cooperates—the face is familiar, but...

He's an old man.

"Papa!" she hugs him, crying. "You weren't supposed to get out until next September. I'm so happy. What happened?"

"Some friends in the West paid to get me released." His eyes are encircled in dark lakes; he's gained quite a bit of weight. He's wearing his old blue sports jacket, but it no longer fits; a paunch fights the zipper.

He seems to read her reaction.

"We didn't have much opportunity to exercise." He looks tired and unshaven, a cocoon in which her real father must be hiding.

"I'm so sorry. Come in, come in." Ulrike backs out of the way, stumbles over a pair of shoes she had neglected to put away, nearly falls. She is awkward, smiling through tears. *Papa doesn't need an invitation into his own flat.* He doesn't seem offended. Her head is boiling over with thoughts.

"Why couldn't they pay sooner?" Ulrike asks.

"I don't know, Uli. These things take negotiation. I've only learned about the whole effort recently. I simply can't bear talking about it today. Tell me, how are you? Is your mother at work? Let me sit down. I need to take all this in. Just the day before yesterday, I thought I had ten more months to go. I'm still not sure *where* I am. Things must have changed. I don't know what exactly. We didn't know anything in there. I still don't.'"

Her father stops, sighs, as if already exhausted by his short speech.

"Sit down, Papa," Ulrike says. "Do you want some tea? Some food?"

"Tea." With a groan, he lowers himself into a chair and rubs his lower back. "They fed us before letting us go. Me and this other prisoner. I don't know his name. We never knew anyone's names. Weren't allowed to run into one another. I wasn't going to talk about it." His expression is shy, guilty, lost.

"I've heard about it, Papa. They kept you isolated, didn't they?" She is crying again while her father's face is overtaken by a vast emptiness as if his ability to emote had been suppressed.

"Yes." His voice, too, is dispassionate.

"*Gott*, Papa. I'm so glad you're back. Let me put that tea on." She busies herself with this simple task.

She's not sure what to ask—what would be helpful—and now that the kettle is on the stove, she has no choice but to sit down opposite her father. "Mama will be so happy. She doesn't know yet, does she?"

"I have no idea."

"So what happens now? Are the Stasi still after us?"

"I don't know. We might as well assume they are. We'll have to keep a low profile." He pauses, his expression removed, his face flat.

A second later, the engaged face returns. "I don't know. I need some time to think about it. To get used to all of this again." He spreads his arms in the air, encompassing everything that to him must feel majestic, everything Ulrike can barely stand. "I couldn't sleep all night after they told me. The excitement caught up with me. Sleep has always been a problem in there. Would you be upset if I rested a while?"

Rest? *He just got here.* She can see how selfish her reaction is. *There will be time to talk.* Her father's face betrays no trace of energy; his eyes are closing.

"Go, rest. We'll talk when Mama gets back. I can't tell you how happy I am, Papa." *Is that the third time I've said it?* From the depths of her sad self, a gigantic grin emerges, and then she tears up again.

It hurts to watch as her father carefully picks up his beat-up body and shuffles over to the bedroom. His determined gait of the former years is undetectable in this stooped figure's tentative steps.

People heal, don't they? They recover. Her father will heal. Ulrike believes it, wants to believe it with all the optimism left in her.

She must believe it.

* * *

"Uli, please pass the sausages." Her father's voice is flat.

The family at the table. *The new, old, unusual configuration. All three of us.* The air is rigid with pain, darkness, and broken hopes.

Before her father went to prison, Ulrike was too young to ask questions about her parents' relationship. They were just a mother and a father, not a couple as such. *Now, after this terrible gap, is there a couple left?*

Her father helps himself to another sausage. He carefully cuts into it, places the piece into his mouth, and chews, an expression of complete and utter happiness on his face. "Nice."

For a moment, he seems to hover in a space outside the room, thinking remote thoughts. *It's hard to believe four years have passed.* Her mother, too, seems ill at ease as she watches her husband eat, an incredulous expression on her face. Barbara has barely started her own meal.

Papa, oh, Papa. All three of us worked against the state in some ways, but he became the designated victim. And now he is different, subdued, as if most of his lifeforce had been sucked out.

Ulrike, too, has grown out of the person she used to be. *It's as if the three of us meet for the first time, and we don't like or understand what we see.* Her head overflows with questions she's afraid to ask. She's heard about sleep deprivation, all sorts of psychological torture, *Das Boot,* a tiny cell with no light. Has her father been subjected to these extreme methods?

"Papa, what did they do to you?" Ulrike's eyes fill with tears.

"Nothing. Nothing special." He avoids eye contact.

"It must have been terrible."

"At first." He sighs; his eyes meet hers for a moment. "Then you get used to it."

"What did they ask you? What did they want to know?"

At this question, her father's face stills once more, as if checked out from this scene and lost in the other reality Ulrike and Barbara are not privy to. He remains there a second or two. "You know, I'm not sure what to say. I'm not ready to talk about it."

* * *

Screams awaken her. For a second, mid-dream, Ulrike assumes the screams are her own—but it's a male voice—her father's. Her mother's conciliatory voice intervenes. Ulrike slips on her bathrobe and hesitantly makes her way to her parents' bedroom. The screaming has stopped—all she can hear are quiet, tense voices. She knocks.

"Uli?" It's her mother.

"Yes."

"Go to bed, dear."

"I'm scared. What's going on? Can I come in?"

A pause, muffled sounds of conversation.

"Okay, come in," her mother says.

A half-moon illuminates the room through the window. Her parents sit on the edge of the bed.

"Your father had a nightmare."

"What was it?" The moment she asks this, Ulrike regrets it.

A muffled sound emanates from the bed—the light is scarce, but now, she can tell that the sound is her father's sobbing. "I can't tell you. I can't tell you."

He sobs, and Barbara holds him. "Come on, lie down. Go back to sleep. It's all okay now. We'll be okay. You're back now. Uli, you go back to bed too."

"Goodnight, Papa," Ulrike says, trying not to cry.

"Goodnight, dear." His voice is strained. "I'm so sorry I woke you up."

"It's okay, Papa. It's okay."

Ulrike remembers his joyful, unabashed smile just a few years earlier, his optimism, his helpful spirit. At this moment, it's clear: not everything can be recovered. *Something in our lives is permanently broken.*

Ulrike closes the door and finds herself in the hallway where no moonlight penetrates—like being inside her own mind, deep in the hopeless space behind the bone.

2002, SAN FRANCISCO

Have you made up your lazy mind yet? Haven't heard from
you in a few weeks, so poor little Brigita is left to wonder if
you're even alive. Great news: I have all the paperwork in
place for my real estate business. We can work together if
you and your Viking decide to come here. It will be like a
commune, except we can actually make a living. There are
so many opportunities here in Berlin. So much everything,
really. Art, music. You will love it, I promise. I miss you,
Uli. Please consider it. From what I keep hearing from you,
life over there is not a piece of cake as you Americanos put
it. Why punish yourself? I could even help you with a place
to live if your parents are not willing, which I'm pretty sure
they are. Of course, you and Peter should visit first and get
an idea of this pageant we call Berlin. Come and visit, you
hear?

Ulrike has been postponing her response. *It would be impossible to
return to Germany now—with the credit card debt, Peter, his job, and
the million projects I've applied for and the few I've committed to.*
How to explain this to the kind and friendly Brigita who has no
experience of this crazy, overpriced world—Brigita the pure, the
one never compromised, neither by the Stasi nor by emigration?
   Ulrike is envious.
   The more she focuses on herself, the less attractive she finds
what she sees. *Is such an existence sustainable? Can I remain so
negative and yet, in some sense, myself?* Depression is an objective
condition—but how to handle the fact that the cynical downer
voice tends to grab hold of the microphone and overpower other
voices?
   Just now, she is empty of energy, incapable of anything, much

less moving to another country, much less moving to that specific terrifying place. Her next session with Sally is not until Thursday, and it's only Sunday. Others get to have a day off, but Ulrike spent all day hammering out stupid-looking web pages, going through uninteresting web design job posts and dubious alternatives. She'd settle for any opportunity that would make her useful to someone willing to pay.

Being useful. That must be what it's all about in this pragmatic little universe of our species—useful, or its opposite: irrelevant, completely and utterly unnecessary. Ulrike closes her laptop. It's dark outside. Peter is running late. She forces herself to get up from the couch and heads straight for the bedroom. She drags off her clothes and climbs under the sheets. *I can't face any more of this day.*

CHAPTER TWENTY-THREE

2003

Ruth was in her bed, Ulrike's client's book in her lap.

I've been so used to blaming my wife all these years that it took sitting down to write this to remember my affair. I knew it had happened; sure, I did. But I was thinking about it as something past. And for Judy, it was a permanent thing. Something broken.

I remember a conversation not long before she left. One of our nearly silent dinners at the very end.

'I've never recovered from that.' Judy threw a quick glance my way. 'It's like your affair, or another one, might be still going on. Or it could start again anytime.'

There wasn't much love left between us. I remember the sadness of that moment.

'Why?' I asked. Dumb question.

'Because since then, I was never able to tell if I could believe you or not. You didn't seem to change much. You were the same person. It's like there were two realities, yours and mine. And I no longer knew what reality I was in.'

I never did have another affair, but in retrospect, I realize Judy couldn't know that. Even I wasn't sure it wouldn't happen. If I was ever tempted, would I be able to resist? Would I want to? I didn't know what to expect of myself. All I've ever had a commitment for has been my work, and that's not a good excuse. I never understood women. My mother was impossible to understand. The way she stepped out of life, it really did a trick on me. But I loved Judy at the start. More than anything in the world. We human beings are a mystery through and through.

Ruth put the book aside. Her eyes were closing.

* * *

Ruth entered the lab in a relatively balanced state. On the way to her bench, she touched Jingfei's shoulder.

"Ruth!" Her colleague's happy grin. It was good being around people.

Ruth sipped her coffee, trying to read her email. *Dad's death, Mother's drinking, the letters, the fear. How did I end up here, in the middle of this decimation? My chemical reaction went astray, its outcome unpredictable. What am I supposed to do with this mess? What would Marie Curie do?*

Through her peripheral vision, Ruth observed a figure leaning over. She turned her head.

"Inspector Rodriguez." She was almost happy to see the Inspector's broad face, his mane of gray hair. Something in her tightened. *Does he have news for me?*

"Good morning, Miss Hanson. Is this a good time to ask you a few questions?"

"Sure, why not? Have a seat."

The Inspector's massive frame looked odd in the chair, as if it hadn't been designed for such a commanding figure. He wore a gray suit and slacks, no tie.

"We've been trying to track your father's whereabouts during the hours preceding his accident."

"Accident?"

"We have to call it that until we have something more solid to confirm foul play. I'm sure you understand. Did you see him the day he died?"

"No, no." Ruth recalled those few days. "I hadn't seen him in a week or so. Why?"

"We've located some footage of your father. It was taken around 11 a.m. that day, at the Berkeley Downtown BART station. What was his reason for being there?"

"Berkeley Downtown?" Ruth thought for a second. "I have no idea. I don't remember him ever going to Berkeley. Or taking BART in the first place. What is he doing? I mean, in the video footage?"

"Nothing. He just talks for a while to some lady, about your age from what we can see. Can't see her face from that camera angle." The Inspector's eyes were friendly, unassuming. "So, it wasn't you?"

"No, no, it wasn't me. I wish!"

"Well, Ma'am, I didn't think so, but it was my responsibility to ask."

Great. So Dad had a lover my age, in addition to being some kind of spy or criminal.

"Why do you think he traveled from Berkeley to El Cerrito?" the Inspector asked.

"I don't know," Ruth said. "Maybe he needed time to think? Looks like my father had secrets he didn't share with us." Suddenly, she was crying—quietly, so as not to disturb her colleagues. "I don't even know why he was in Berkeley," she mumbled through her tears.

"I'm sorry to upset you, Miss Hanson. You've been very helpful. He shouldn't have kept secrets from you and your mother."

How nice of him to confirm this. Is that a cop's responsibility? With a typical polite nod, Inspector Rodriguez rose. Ruth admired his confident posture as she watched him walk toward the exit. She was left with more of her father's mess. A mess she and her mother were stuck with for the rest of their lives. Their family legacy, Ruth's inheritance.

Her coffee was getting cold but remained tasty, the bitterness welcome on her tongue. *No going wrong with coffee as long as it's strong enough. Molecules don't lie.* Was nothing beyond the molecular level reliable?

Pushing someone down the train tracks would be easy at a station, but how did one end up on the rails in the middle of nowhere? *Am I the next to be found in El Cerrito? Is Mom?* She wished she'd told Rodriguez about the threats.

Ruth drank the rest of her coffee and leapt off her chair for a refill. A couple of colleagues milled about in the kitchen; small talk followed. Ruth could tell her coworkers would love to ask about her visitor—but they resisted, acting shifty instead, as if uncomfortable being there.

"It's just the cop, you know." She shrugged. "The one working on my father's case. Nothing new. Just more questions."

A mix of sighs and brief compassionate statements ensued. The

A. MOLOTKOV

kitchen cleared within a minute of Ruth's arrival. *No one wants to discuss my troublesome new reality.*

Ruth checked herself. *The two things may have been unrelated.* The others had secured their coffee and snacks and returned to their respective benches or desks. *The lab's interpersonal dynamic doesn't revolve around me.*

CHAPTER TWENTY-FOUR

The family has gathered around the small kitchen table, discussing the recent developments. No one is afraid to talk about these things anymore—the feeling is that the regime's collapse is irreversible.

"What do you think is going to happen?" Ulrike studies her parents' faces.

Peaceful Revolution is in full swing in East Germany. Prager Strasse glows, lit up with passion. Emotions have reached a boiling point. Ulrike is twenty, a good age for change.

"Nothing's going to happen," her father says. "It'll be okay."

Most other communist states have given up, and the Soviet Union is well into its fortunate self-destruction named perestroika. Here, the protesters have been gathering for days.

"Don't be so sure," Barbara says. "The Stasi have been expecting this. They could shoot down the whole demonstration and be rid of all the dissidents at once."

"They won't dare—things are beyond that point." *Surprisingly, Papa sounds more positive.* "The system can't survive—it simply can't. The USSR is the only reason it has lasted as long as it has. With that piece of shit broken, Honecker is bound to see he'd be in trouble if people got killed."

"You assume these bastards are logical." Barbara is manic and unsmiling. "They are not. Honecker is a crazy man. Mielke is even worse. No one knows if they are going to make logical choices or just blow the whole thing up."

Ulrike knows as much about Erich Mielke, Honecker's right-hand man, and the Stasi Chief. Still, she is full of optimism.

"I agree with you, Mama. These original socialists make the line between true belief and con so blurry it's hard to tell if they sincerely trust any of the shit they keep funneling down our throats. But I trust that they won't put themselves at risk by doing anything too drastic. They know the tide is turning. Now, they have to be very careful."

2003, BERKELEY

Dietrich's house on Grant is happy in the sun, resting as all good houses rest. *Dietrich is unlikely to be home.* Ulrike didn't bother to call.

Dietrich opens the door, disproving the theory of his absence. Ulrike finds herself disappointed. She mourns that loss of privacy she'd expected—the luxury of waiting. *Hadn't realized that Dietrich's habit of tardiness was a good thing, a welcome break.*

Dietrich grins, the asshole—he looks genuinely happy to see her. *Admittedly, he is sexy in a pair of faded jeans and a dark gray shirt.* His arms are already out for her, and she goes in for the hug but not the kiss, which is not lost on Dietrich. He pulls away and examines her incredulously.

"What's going on, babe?" His voice is low; he clears his throat.

"We need to talk. Can we go inside?"

"Sure thing."

The sun dances on the wood floor and the tall ceiling as the birch tree outside sways in the wind. Ulrike can't see the tree from the door, but she knows what causes the light's animation. *It's important to notice details at times like this, even if the memory is not going to be accurate.*

"A beer?" Dietrich follows her to the kitchen.

"Sure—why not."

She plops in the chair next to the elegant round table, a lovely piece of furniture with its intricate mushroom-shaped base covered in wood designs. Dietrich hands her a bottle of Hefeweizen, one of his few German preferences. *What a fake German he is. Not that he's ever tried to go for authentic German-ness. I'm a fake German myself. I grew up in a make-believe sub-Germany that no longer exists.*

"What's up?" Dietrich places the beer before her. He doesn't bother to get a glass, and Ulrike doesn't care enough to get up and get one.

She takes a sip. "I can't do this anymore."

"Can't do what?"

"Dude, don't be obtuse. This. This affair."

"Why? Did he find out?" A mix of concern and excitement on Dietrich's face, as if the real adventure of their affair would start only if Peter learned about it.

"No, he didn't find out. It's me. I can't do it anymore."

"Why not?" Dietrich looks sincerely stunned.

"It just doesn't feel right anymore. I've been feeling terrible about doing this to Peter. He doesn't deserve it. He works overtime, he pays most of our bills—and here I am."

"Doesn't he treat you like shit?" Dietrich takes a swig of his beer, lights a cigarette, and holds the pack out to Ulrike. The lighter's click-clack brings a welcome pause.

"I have told you some things that may not be fair." Ulrike frowns as she concentrates on stating this as precisely as she can muster. "He can be harsh on me sometimes, but it's often because of something *I* missed. I've given you a simplistic idea of our life. I needed an excuse. But now, I know this can't go on, just can't."

Dietrich stares blankly from across the table, a lost child unequipped to understand. Ulrike takes another gulp of her beer, burps. Dietrich gets up from his chair and approaches her from behind. His hands on her shoulders, gently rubbing.

"It's okay," he says.

"Is it?"

"Yes." Dietrich's right hand descends to the top of her right breast and rests a second. Two fingers carefully slide around her nipple. The touch is right and wrong: her body wants it, but her mind does not. *Or is it the other way around? Who can tell the difference anymore? Isn't the brain another body part?* "Want to do it one last time?"

Dietrich's left hand mimics the right—it's so easy to go with this —this man's hands are good at exciting her—on any other day, she would have gone along. *I can't, I just can't.* As soon as she thinks this, Dietrich's hands feel wooden on her breasts, and she gently takes each in her own and moves them off. Dietrich's arms hover over her for a few seconds, steeped in indecision.

"So that's it, then?" His voice is matter-of-fact.

"It has to be. I'm sorry."

"What's changed?"

As Dietrich awaits her answer, Ulrike is lost. *What is it that has changed? Anything? Everything?*

"A lot of shit has happened to me lately. Maybe some of it didn't have to happen? What if I made it happen by being careless or dumb or whatever it is that I am? Something in my life is not working. More than one thing. I need to cut my losses, apologize, and make a simpler life for myself."

"I thought *this* was the thing that was working," Dietrich says with a coy grin, pointing toward the bedroom with its perpetually unmade bed.

"Shut up, bastard!" Ulrike can't help smiling. "It was working, and I'll miss it, and I'm sorry. I'll remember you fondly, as they say."

"Let's drink to that." Dietrich raises his beer. "Give me a call if you change your mind." He sounds unengaged, loss barely registering among the many nuances his voice conveys, a confident smile still there on his damn face. *What was I expecting? Intimacy? Is that what she has with Peter, with herself? Does intimacy exist?*

Ulrike feels as if she is viewing a vast city from a great height, and all its streets and squares and railroads are right there before her, except the city is her life, and all the infrastructure is utterly broken. She feels sad and empty about it—but also hopeful. *Infrastructure can be rebuilt if one is capable of rebuilding.*

CHAPTER TWENTY-FIVE

2003

The blue house on Russian Hill looked the same as usual. A narrow three-story box with a pleasing angle of the roof, it had contained the family for their eighteen years as a trio until Ruth went to college. Now the house had become a solitary dwelling.

No response. It was after 6 p.m. *Where can Mother possibly be at this hour? A stupid question. She could be anywhere, a thousand places: a walk, a store, a coffee shop. People's lives contain billions of unnoticed moments, unobserved motions, accidental and insignificant moves.*

Ruth was worried about her mother—and mad at her for being a solipsistic drunk.

She rang again and waited. Her eye to the keyhole, she saw no movement.

She heard something.

Music.

Ruth rang again, several times in a row, with extended pressing each time. No reaction. She hammered the door with her fist, then looked around to check if anyone could see her making so much noise. An elderly couple on the porch across the street contemplated her with remote curiosity.

How annoying, this situation. Just what one would expect from Mother.

Ruth would not accept this solitary music. Something in this formula didn't connect. Her mother was pedantic enough to pause a song if she walked downstairs to pour herself a drink. She'd have to be in a peculiar frame of mind to leave the house with music still playing. *No, no, she's home.*

Ruth unlocked the door with her own key. Here it was, the music, subdued but clearly audible, coming from upstairs—a tango. *Astor Piazzolla?* Ruth followed the sound to her parents' bedroom.

Linda lay sprawled in bed, a martini glass in her hand, her pink PJs sullen at the edges. Her eyes were closed, but she was not asleep, as evidenced by her foot tapping air in time with the music. Ruth stood there a few moments, observing. Without opening her eyes, her mother lifted her head from the pillow, brought the glass to her lips, and took a sip. She sighed with relief, as if this particular sip were precisely what had lacked in her life.

"Mother!" Ruth said.

Linda stirred, her eyes opening to 75% capacity.

"Ruthie, dear. What...What are you doing here? You should have called. Would you like a martini?" She stirred as if to rise and follow up on her offer, but then hesitation washed over her face. With a dismissive wave, she abandoned the move.

"You're *really* drinking again! You said you'd stop." *I should have checked up on her earlier.* Ruth felt defeated, incapable of helping herself or others.

"Just a couple...couple of fucking drinks won't hurt anyone." Linda gesticulated emphatically, precipitating a small spill from her martini glass. Some of the liquid darkened the light blue cover over her legs.

"That's not what happened last time, Mother."

"Last time? Which last time? Last time my husband got involved in something fishy and got killed? Or the time before that?"

How infuriating. Ruth's face was burning, her head about to explode. *I wish there were a legal way to dispose of one's mother.* "Dad's death is not an excuse for this. Please pull yourself together. I simply don't have the capacity to worry about you on top of all the other stuff. You can't just drink yourself into oblivion and add to all my problems. Not to mention that I love you, and it breaks my heart to see you like this."

"Oh, yes, all the other stuff." Her mother grinned, hanging on to something earlier in Ruth's statement, something Ruth no longer remembered exactly. How typical. "There are days when drinking does you no good, no good at all. I'll give you that." After the initial warmup, Linda's annunciation was improving. "And then, there are days when drinking is just the thing that makes life tolerable, helps you get through the day. Don't worry, dear. I'm a big girl. I can decide for myself what's good for me."

I shouldn't have gone down this path. Arguing will get us nowhere. A prescription may have been what Linda needed, but Linda didn't believe in 'good mood pills.' Ruth had also proposed the notion of therapy, her mother's response a firm "I'm not paying someone to talk to me."

"You know what I mean," Ruth said softly.

"Listen, dear..." Linda gulped down the rest of her drink. "You can't tell me what to do. Now that your father is gone, what do I have to live for? What? So please leave me the fuck alone." With shaking hands, she lit a cigarette, inhaled vigorously, and blew the smoke in Ruth's direction.

The nauseating stench of this most unnecessary concoction filled Ruth's lungs. How odd that so many human beings were willing to give up their lives for the small nicotine molecule,

$C_{10}H_{14}N_2$, with its lightweight hydrogen, vaporous like the smoke itself. Her mother had been a smoker in her youth. *This reunion with nicotine comes with the territory: alcohol softens one's brain, mars judgment.*

Something else about Mother's statement. 'With your father gone, what do I have to live for?' There it was, her mother's life, abdicated for someone she didn't even like—and now meaningless without him.

"I need you, Mother." Ruth was exasperated, all certainty and optimism drained by her mother's impenetrable negative space. She was unable to keep a balanced voice. "Please don't kill yourself."

"Nonsense, dear. No one is killing herself. I'm just having a little drink, thassall."

"Which little drink? Your fifth? Your tenth?"

"As far as I'm concerned, it's no one else's business, so leave me the hell alone. How many times do I have to say it?" With some effort, Linda rose from her bed, picked up her empty glass lying next to her. Through the bedroom door, Ruth could see her hold firmly to the handrail as she slowly and deliberately descended, the smoking cigarette in her mouth, the empty glass in her left hand.

Ruth remained in the bedroom, paralyzed, reluctant to follow her mother around the house. She heard Linda's shuffling steps downstairs. The opening refrigerator door. The clinking of ice against glass. More steps. More clinking. *This is taking a century. Mother is in a zone, on her own time.*

Linda reentered, a half-filled pitcher in her right hand, the cigarette in her left. A precariously long column of ash hung off its tip. Ruth considered mentioning the cigarette but thought better of it. Linda refilled her glass and placed the pitcher on the bedside table. She grabbed the glass and took a vigorous gulp. Her awkward transition back into bed sent ashes scattering over the pillow. She didn't seem to notice.

"So you're just going to keep drinking?" Ruth asked.

"If you don't mind." Another gulp.

By now Linda's eyes were at 50%. *Only a few more drinks to go before she passes out. My presence would have a detrimental effect.* Ruth rose and walked out without another word.

* * *

Ruth shared the aggravating story of her encounter with Linda, and Peter listened, followed, asked questions. They fell into an easy back-and-forth. Ruth felt relaxed and comfortable with this man. Peter, too, seemed to enjoy himself. The barista at Saint Frank's already knew their names. Their second round of caffeinated drinks steamed before them. Peter ordered a slice of cheesecake; Ruth was tempted.

"I was reading about this guy, Albert Hoffman." Peter smiled. "Do you know him?" His face was sincere, inquisitive.

"I know *about* him."

"Dude's ninety or something. Sounds like he enjoys his results with LSD in more ways than one."

Ruth scanned her memory. "He developed a few other hallucinogens if I'm not mistaken."

"Have you ever tried acid?"

Is this a trap? Would I compromise my position if I say yes? Immediately, Ruth recognized how paranoid this was. She'd truly become something in the last few months. *Everyone has tried LSD.*

"A few times, back at school," she said. "You?"

"Same thing. It was fun, I must admit. So, listen." Peter's smile was broad, open. "You're a chemist. Would you be able to synthesize it?"

Ruth couldn't help laughing. "Right! I'd blow myself up for drugs and rock-n-roll." It felt good to crack up at the expense of chemistry.

"You could do it at work." He grinned. "After hours. You could even put in for overtime."

"Nostalgic for your student days?" Ruth felt at home with Peter's sense of humor and his acceptance of her own careless remarks.

"To be honest, mine is a drug-free job. It sucks, I know." He made a funny grimace. "They test us every few months. I won't be able to enjoy your acid. Maybe when I retire."

"Acid doesn't show up in tests. You should know this by now."

Both collapsed into laughter as if Peter's mistake were the most hilarious omission known to humankind.

"I don't know if I could benefit from acid at this point in my life." Ruth sighed. "It takes too long. I don't have the time."

* * *

They stood outside the coffee shop. After three hours of non-stop conversation, Ruth was grateful to this man. *He made room in his day for my complaints. A good listener.* True, she'd also listened to some of his own guilty conscience talk on account of Ulrike and his religious adoptive parents. They'd discussed Ruth's parents too. It was good to talk, just talk.

Ruth was impressed—and yes, quite attracted to this man. Without any thinking on her part, she wrapped her arms around him. Their lips worked their way around one another—her skin came alive all at once. The two of them were subatomic particles drawn together.

Then they were in Peter's car, a short ride to his place. They barely spoke. They kissed on the stairs as they ascended to the second floor. They kissed while Peter unlocked the apartment door, which caused the unlocking to take an exceptional amount of time.

High ceilings, tall windows, wood floor, light blue walls. The layout floated before Ruth's eyes without fully registering. The thought of Ulrike hovered in the background. Somehow, this made the whole thing even more exciting. Ruth's body tingled; her heart slammed against all of her from inside. *What would Sarah think of me with this Black man?*

"Can I offer you a drink?" Peter was out of breath.

"Please."

"Give me a minute." Peter separated himself and made a move toward the kitchen.

Ruth's arms fell at her sides like dead weights.

"Never mind." She reached after him and pulled him against her body. "We'll have drinks later."

They made their way to the bedroom, kissing, already dragging off the most removable of clothes. Red curtains fluttered in the draft from a slightly open window. Where Peter's hands touched, her skin reacted with an electric response. *Good thing Peter thought of a condom; I'm much too distracted.* She couldn't remember feeling such desire with Vladko, with any of her small group of former lovers.

The two of them didn't make it to the bed, but stood, her back leaning on the wall. Then he lowered his body against her, was inside her. She gasped, her arms around his neck.

"You okay?" Peter pulled away to see her face.

"Yes, yes. Don't stop."

He was in great shape, his muscles firm, inevitable against her, nothing wiggly between the two of them. His touch rang through her body like hydrogen and oxygen, joining.

CHAPTER TWENTY-SIX

Martin Luther King Jr. Park on her left beckons Ulrike with its small playground. *Who cares if a few junkies enjoy the space too? It's a block-sized park, and there's enough room in it. But it's sad, too.* No point in lingering. She casts a final look at the shabby sandbox, the brightly painted carriage on springs—these are the Berkeley images she has taken in on a few dozen occasions, images that have become habits, become her life. *My dumb nonsense of a life.*

Ulrike enters the futuristic round building of the BART station, slides her pass, and descends to the platform. *The day feels unreal.* A few people congregate in the middle of the station, but she is drawn to a concrete bench farther down with plenty of available seats at this time of day.

Someone is already there, an elderly man wearing nondescript pensioner clothes: brown pants and a white polo shirt. A warn brown leather briefcase is next to him. He looks safe. As Ulrike approaches, he turns his head and offers a warm smile.

Ulrike can't help but smile back. "Hi."

She sits down.

"Hello." His voice is low and pleasant. He regards her with a kind face. "You look like something important is happening in your life."

A preposterous thing to say to a stranger—but what the hell, I don't mind engaging him, especially today. The man's face is tired, the dark shadows under his eyes immense.

"How can you tell?" She enjoys talking to strangers—these brief encounters often carry more honesty than well-practiced conversations between people who know each other.

"I pay attention." His tone is unassuming. "But let me introduce myself first. David. David Conrad." He offers his hand; she shakes it.

"Ulrike Schumacher. Nice to meet you, David."

David's friendly eyes examine her. His face is thin with high cheekbones, a feminine delicacy combined with firm chin and lips. *A good-looking face.* The BART station around them is largely unoccupied. With its sections of brick wall and its levitating ceilings, it's a time machine transporting Ulrike into an unknown future she is unprepared for.

"I hope I wasn't being presumptuous. It's quite a day for me too. That's why I asked." David Conrad's expression is open and interested.

On a day like this, full of peculiar unpredictabilities, I might as well let chance have its way. "You were being presumptuous, but that's okay with me. What's wrong with your day?"

"I'm meeting someone in an hour." He shrugs. "It may end up being a tough one."

"A friend?"

"A colleague."

"What happened?"

David thinks a while. *Was my question too direct again?*

"I decided to retire, and my colleague doesn't like the idea. He thinks I have too much skill to retire."

"But it's your choice in the end, isn't it?"

Ulrike is no expert in matters of choice. *It takes me longer to decide anything than it would take flowers to bloom on the moon.*

"Of course. It's my choice." He nods. "And you? What's wrong with your day?"

"I just broke up with my lover." Ulrike is surprised by her honesty, by the ease of it.

There must be something about David's face and his predicament. Difficult to imagine anyone with a face like this, lying. Ulrike is sick and tired of maneuvering through a world filled with conspiracies. *For fuck's sake, it's time for a life free of secrets.*

"You did?" David's eyebrows go up.

"I couldn't do it to my husband anymore. And to myself. I know stopping it doesn't make it go away. I know this, but still..." Ulrike feels sharply present in the moment, the conversation's essential pull on her like gravity. *It's important to express this as clearly as possible.* "I don't know why I started this affair in the first place. I was mad but mad at myself more than anyone."

"I understand." David nods. "Feelings build up—things we don't take time to articulate." He frowns and considers something. "Our stories are not too different. I broke up with a lady friend recently, and I can't stand myself for the affair."

"So you're married too?" Ulrike smiles.

"Yes."

"How long?"

"Forty-four years."

"Wow." Ulrike is overwhelmed by the number. It could be a rocket that propels a happy couple to a higher meaning of life or an anchor that drowns them in a dull, unfair arrangement. "Only six for Peter and me, and I'm already unsure where it's going."

"In these things, you're never sure." David pauses, looking down the tunnel. "How did it start? The affair, I mean?"

"Oh, it doesn't matter. Just me, being lost."

"Lost? Yes. Yes. Myself, I kind of stumbled into mine. We worked together, she and I. And the work was intense sometimes. I shouldn't be surprised that it became emotional. We ended up having more to share than my wife and I did. My wife, she's an odd bird anyway. I don't know if I've ever understood her. When we met, she was a puzzle I hoped to crack someday. That kept it interesting. But I never did crack it." He shifts and thinks about something for a moment. "Still, it's my fault. You mentioned choice earlier. I got myself into that by choice."

"Let's drink to choice." Ulrike raises an imaginary glass.

With a respectful nod, David returns the gesture. They make a move to clink.

"What kind of work do you do?" Ulrike asks.

David frowns, examines something above her. "I'll tell you, but only on one condition."

"What condition?"

"It's for your safety. Don't turn your head." David's voice is very calm. "Behind you is a BART video camera. Right now, it's getting my face, but not yours. It will be impossible to identify you without a frontal view. If anyone is looking for me, you won't become involved. I'm not saying they are; it's very unlikely. I'm just being careful. Deal?"

"Deal," Ulrike fires back. *I should be scared, but I feel intrigued— something to take my mind off the emptiness of my own life.*

"You asked me about my work. I work with secrets. I find things out. In some cases, I hide them. I work for an organization that exists for the good of the American people, or so it is assumed. Not officially, you see. I'm off the books."

"Are you a spy?" Ulrike doesn't know whether to laugh or to

run. But she's in a public space. She's supposed to fear spies, but she feels no fear.

An embarrassed smile appears on David's face. "Call it what you want."

"If this were true, you would never tell me."

A city-bound train arrives with its noise and its small bundle of disembarking passengers. *I'll skip this one.*

"You're right. Normally I wouldn't tell." He stares as if deciding how much to reveal. "Today, I'm at the end of my rope, and you have an open face."

"Why did you decide to retire?" Ulrike feels a concerned frown on her face. *For some reason, I'm really interested in this man's situation.*

"I was no longer happy with what we were doing. We trained and armed people who turned against us on 9/11. When I was young, it was easier to explain away all the stuff that happened in South America." He pauses. "We've made bigger cracks in the world than anyone else."

"Bigger cracks in the world?" Ulrike holds these odd words on her tongue. "I'm from East Germany. It's certainly a crack, but I'm not sure who to blame. It's no longer even a country as such—just a poor province of the real Germany."

David laughs, briefly. "Your former country wasn't the best place to be, that's true. How does this make you feel, seeing it gone?"

"I'm happy that the regime is over. The best outcome we could have hoped for. And my parents at least tried to do something about it." Ulrike considers this, the fingers of her right hand bothering her left thumb, a tick she's still trying to get rid of. "Me...I just waited until things changed and then I left. I couldn't bother to stay behind and try to fix it." She hears disdain for herself in her own voice.

"Fixing things takes a special mindset. Not everyone has it, nor should they have to. You didn't break anything, so how can you be responsible for fixing it?"

It's nice to imagine that I haven't broken anything, anything at all.

"And you?" Ulrike is not sure what exactly she is asking.

"People in our profession burn out, you know. We should meddle less."

"Let's drink to meddling less."

Once more, they perform an imaginary clink, imaginary glasses light in their hands.

1990, DRESDEN

It's dinnertime at the Schumachers' flat. Fading light crawls through the windows while the tree outside becomes more of a dark mass, less a collection of branches. The kitchen is warm and cozy, lit in a glow of better days.

In a span of just a few months, the unimaginable is true. Dead is the evil empire most East Germans expected to last forever. No more Berlin Wall. Open borders. Western goods. Families are reuniting, and many are leaving the East.

It had never occurred to Ulrike that the two sides might join together to form a single country. She'd expected the GDR to stay there, half a century behind, a lesson to others willing to flirt with revolutionary ideologies. *I'm ready to vomit just from remembering life in a society where everyone is supposed to agree. My country was a nasty pimple on Europe's ass long enough.*

Hundreds of Berlin flats sit abandoned, available for squatting and wild parties. Brigita has gone for a week and plans to move there. But to Ulrike, Berlin is just another part of the gray world. She wants to be as far from all of it as possible. *How can I feel safe here?*

Her father has cooked steak, lean and tender, the likes of which had not been available in East Germany until this year. As the family chews and enjoys the luxury of normalcy, an unexpected conclusion bursts forth in Ulrike's mind—the sum of all her thoughts from recent months.

"I've decided to move to America." She grabs her water glass and takes a big gulp. Her body feels warm from the correctness of her decision.

"America?" Barbara repeats blankly. "What are you talking about?"

"I'm tired of this place, *Mutter.* I'm suffocating here. We have all the freedoms now, but no one has any real freedom in their minds. No one knows what to do. They're too happy to play the victims. Don't you feel it?"

"What are you talking about, Uli?" Barbara's eyes burn with indignation. "We can get out, travel, read all the books we want. And you're suffocating? How can it be? I don't understand." Barbara's half-clenched hands are claws around her face. "That's what we've fought for, isn't it? Günter, what do you think?"

"America?" Her father lays down his knife and fork, and the utensils clatter against the plate's white surface. "Darling, your mother's right. Things are just beginning to go well here. What's all this business about America?"

In her corner of the family triangle, Ulrike feels utterly alone.

"Look at what this place has done to our family, to you. Do you ever talk to Uncle Franz anymore? All we have left are big questions: what to do, how to fix the problems, how to be one country instead of two enemies. I'm tired of all that. I want to go to a functional place that's been around a while and has taken care of its problems. I'm not good at solving political issues, you see."

Too many thoughts bubble up in Ulrike's head, but after sharing her unexpected decision, she feels less anxious. She helps herself to another portion of steak with fried potatoes.

"United States, for god's sake. How will you get there? You need a visa, something." Barbara flicks her fingers in the air as if seeking more precise terminology.

"I've heard that getting a residence would be difficult unless I go to college. Wouldn't you like me to go to college in the States? If I decide to stay, I can help you move there too."

"Unbelievable." Barbara looks astonished, while Günter's face remains neutral.

"Maybe I need to leave to regain affection for Germany." She thinks for a moment. "To be honest, the affection may never return. *Return*—that's not even the right word. I've never felt any affection. Since I was a child, I've lived amidst people who hate the place."

Barbara is motionless, tears running down her cheeks. *If I leave, Papa will be all alone in caring for Mutter's mood swings. Once again, he will pay the price while I enjoy a cool new life in the States. I can't leave, can I?*

But how can I stay if I can't imagine a future in this sad world?

CHAPTER TWENTY-SEVEN

2003

Ruth's eyes opened to see red. *Peter must have drawn the curtains last night.* She lay on her side, her hand neatly tucked under the red pillow.

She felt anxious and excited, in a dangerous experiment with components that could blow up or produce an exceptional outcome. The two of them had stayed up till three, making love and talking.

An electric bus powerline hovered in the window. *Hard to find a view of San Francisco that doesn't include these hanging testaments to electricity. Edison would be proud.* Ruth slowly turned onto her back and tilted her head to examine Peter's sleeping body. His breath was steady, his broad muscular chest beautiful with its smooth skin. His face looked content, open to the world.

For a moment, Ruth felt lucky to be here, like this. She was horny again, a state infrequent in the last few months. Then she felt anxious. *What am I doing? Barely six months after Ulrike's death,*

Peter isn't ready for this. I've insinuated myself into his life. That word kept coming back, "insinuated."

Ruth was tempted to bolt out of bed, throw her clothes on, run —run before Peter woke. Instead, she decided to wait it out to see how the morning might unfold. *I have nothing to lose.* Peter stirred as if the intensity of her gaze had interrupted his repose. His eyes, quick to open, found her. The expression on his face was of—joy. But his eyes were sad also.

"Good morning." Peter's hand casually touched her stomach and remained there.

"Good morning."

"Were you awake long?"

"Not long. Just five or ten minutes. I was watching you."

"Hmm...I'm flattered. I don't think anyone has watched me before." His hand moved a half inch down.

"Didn't Ulrike watch you?"

The moment Ruth said it, she knew how wrong the question was. So did Peter. His hand withdrew.

"Oh, shit! I'm so sorry. I didn't mean it, Peter."

A few breaths passed.

"I guess both of us might need a day or two to digest this." Peter's voice was flat. "It's my first time since...since she died. I don't know what that's supposed to mean. I'm sorry."

Through the cracks between the red curtains, the gray sky looked uninviting.

"Yes." Ruth's voice came out weak, meaningless. *My stupid question has ruined everything.*

"I'll make coffee." Peter frowned.

No matter what else happened today, coffee was an agreeable idea, even in the middle of a broken situation. *I've contaminated the experiment.* Ruth lay in the fetal position, wishing time would stop. Peter got out of bed. He was naked and not shy about it. *He has no reason to be.* As he started the coffee machine, Ruth watched him through the bedroom door. *I'll remember this: last night, this beautiful naked man.*

"Almost ready." Peter held something up in the air to show her. It was half of a coffee cake. Ruth gave a thumbs up.

She wasn't concerned about being nude either. She'd thought she would be. *My legs still look good, and my body is in a reasonable shape.* She took her time putting on her bra before she found her panties in the pile of clothes discarded by the bed. Peter's eyes were on her, but she couldn't quite read his expression.

She quickly put on the rest of her clothes and joined Peter at the kitchen table. The coffee was strong and reliable. *Such a relief considering what some people mistake for coffee.* It was good to have the drink to occupy herself with.

"I'm sorry," Ruth repeated.

"Don't be." Peter's voice was impassive.

The coffee cake helped with the silence. Ruth felt resigned to the loss of their shared spark. *I wish he'd get over it, but he seems stuck on my awful faux pas.* She was numb rather than sad. *Something happened, and now we are on this side of it.* She couldn't change that any more than she could reverse her father's death.

"Do you have to go to work?" Ruth asked, just to say something.

"Yes, in forty minutes or so. What are you going to do?"

"Work." She shrugged.

They were silent for a while.

"I need some time to think about this." Peter's voice was shaky. He avoided eye contact. "I'm sorry."

"I understand. I probably should go. You must get ready for work and all that." She desperately wanted Peter to say, 'No, stay.'

"Sure," he replied instead. "I need to take a shower."

"Thanks for the coffee."

"Thanks for being here." Still, his voice was off, his eyes elusive. Ruth rose and picked up her bag. Peter didn't move.

"Bye."

"Bye, Ruth. It was fun." Peter approached her halfway and hovered there by the table as if tempted to embrace her but uncommitted.

Fun? Is that what it was?

Trying to keep tears from showing up too soon, Ruth walked to the door and cast another glance at Peter's hesitant posture, the red curtains. *This glimpse of Ulrike's life.* She floated down two flights of stairs without noticing.

She walked out the front door and stood there, mortified, startled by the street's insistent voice.

1991

Ruth sat on the couch, missing Sarah, who was getting her master's in political science at NYU. Ruth took a voluminous hit from the glass bong she'd inherited from her friend. It was the end of June, a day off her part-time lab job, with nothing much to do. Ruth's thoughts had already begun wandering, drugs or no drugs.

She was envious, too. *New York City.* She'd been a few times, and she had to admit: the place challenged the city-ness of San Francisco. New York's vast subway lines, countless colleges, numerous labs—the city's busy millions—all of that amounted to an intoxicating place to be.

Her thoughts returned to chemistry, her agitated mind scanning the gallery of the scientists who had impressed her most. *All the Nobel prizes in the Curie family, all the early deaths from radiation.* The health risks hadn't been discovered yet. *If they knew their research would shorten their lives, would they have gone on with it?*

Of course. There was no doubt in Ruth's mind. Who wouldn't give up some years, an abstract number, to amount to something, to contribute to science? She'd gotten into a phone argument with Sarah about this.

"I don't know how you can sit there and think about chemicals all day. Things are really bad out there, you know. Oppression, poverty. I don't need to explain it to you. Don't you want to join the fight?"

"Not all of us are here to fight." Ruth paused to think. "Not in the same way. I'm not saying it's not worth it—but I'm better at something else. Science. If I play my life right, my main contribution is going to be in that area. I'm still voting next year, you know." She sounded apologetic, even to herself. "And I donate to ACLU."

"Of course. Relax. I don't mean to challenge you." Sarah laughed on the other end of the line. "I love you, darling. I know you're in it because that's who you are."

What a self-contained way to put it, like a steady molecule. Ruth missed her friend's exuberant personality and boundless energy, her sharp intelligence. She hadn't made any other good friends. *Why?* At twenty-two, she'd come close to settling into what might be called an ambitious life, one that didn't leave room for much else. She'd applied for several master's programs. Her thoughts focused on the future, but she wanted to learn more before she was ready to enter it. She appreciated the time to think about the topics the smartest chemists pondered—to consider them more broadly than a particular job would allow. She needed a few more years to catch up in the field.

Ten years from now, it will be 2001. Perhaps by then, I'll have my PhD and a job at a high-end research lab. A phone call interrupted Ruth's career planning.

"Hello, Ruthie." Her dad's voice. "How are you?"

Since her mother's detour into rehab, the family situation had become ever more fragile. Ruth viscerally rejected time with her parents, who could barely spend five minutes in the same room without an argument. The more years separated Ruth from her family dynamic, the more she realized how poisoned her childhood had been. *Most other people had much more functional families. Most.*

"What's up, Dad? What do you need?" She knew he hadn't called to chat.

"I want you to check on your mother. She's getting gloomy— and she's been difficult. I'm concerned for her."

"And so you call me?"

"Yes, Ruthie. She might listen to you. She sure as hell wouldn't do me the same honor."

"Why should she?" Ruth was irritated at her father's incongruous demands.

"What do you mean, darling?"

"I mean, you're full of it. I'm sorry, Dad, but we both know you have secrets you've never shared. And you can't just call me every so often to have me fix it all for you. You must own up to some of this shit. Pardon my language." Now that Ruth had said it, she felt tense, her heart pumping with excessive determination—but she felt a sense of liberation too. *I'm no longer voiceless with my father.*

"What's gotten into you, Ruthie?" His voice on the other end of the line was hard to read.

"What's gotten into me? Really? That's all you have to say?" She waited a while, enough for her father to offer something substantial. But the silence lingered, meaningless and uncomfortable. "Why don't you call me back when you have something to say?"

Ruth slammed the red receiver into the cradle, shocked by the way she'd just spoken to her father but also excited, regretting nothing. *Sarah would be proud of me.*

2003

From across the street, Golden Gate Park frowned at Ruth in the glow of the setting sun. Two days had passed, and Peter hadn't called.

Why should he?

Why shouldn't he?

What about Dad and the secret he's made of his life?

Jerk.

Ruth was surprised to find herself thinking this way about her father. Then, she wasn't.

Once the sun started its dive into the Pacific, she broke down and called Peter. She got the voice mail.

"Peter. It's me. It's Ruth. I'm...well, I just wanted to see how you were doing. I'm not sure if things ended on a good note—in any case, I just wanted to say I'm sorry. And, you know, call me if you want to talk or anything." She paused, desperately scratching her brain for something else, some important detail she may have missed. "Well, I guess that's it. So, thanks." She paused again for just a second or two. "Talk to you later."

Ruth hung up, defeated, her eyes blind to the world around her.

* * *

By the next morning, Peter still hadn't called. *Precisely what I had feared. And precisely what I deserve.* Until she'd made a fool of herself and called the night before, she could have convinced herself that Peter was still a possibility.

Ruth finished her coffee and picked up her purse. She walked briskly to the bus stop, buttoning up her red jacket. The morning was cold. The ocean's gray invaded Fulton Street, obscuring the houses closer to the waterfront. The view did nothing to cheer her up, nor did the ride to work.

The lab was quiet, the kitchen empty. Someone had already made a pot of coffee. Ruth filled her red mug, enjoying the cheerful aroma. An open box of donuts sat on the kitchen table.

Using a napkin, Ruth grabbed a jelly donut and bit off a third. *Delicious.* She walked to her bench with the coffee mug in one hand and the rest of the donut in the other, still chewing. She positioned the donut on the benchtop, then changed her mind and headed to the kitchen again, her manner steady and confident. She grabbed one more donut, a double chocolate.

Back at her bench, Ruth placed the new donut next to her first trophy. For half a minute, she admired the picture: a cup of coffee, a donut, and two-thirds. *This formula can make anyone's day better.*

Whatever happened to Jingfei and that man she met on the cruise?

Ruth knew she should ask. She had other things to do. She'd start by calibrating the centrifuge for a series of tests. Working in a well-established environment always calmed her, even if the tests were routine.

Ruth opened a few files to go over her results from last week. The numbers on the screen were interesting—a pattern emerging, even if she couldn't explain it yet. She considered the effect of temperature. She thought of Peter. She went back to the project, but it was too late. Peter was on her mind, his tall, muscular body crashing with hers, his beautiful, soft skin.

CHAPTER TWENTY-EIGHT

Ulrike's seat is near the airplane's ass—she's among the last passengers to get out. As she makes her way down the aisle, the cleaning crew gets ready for the next flight.

"Thank you for flying with us." The middle-aged flight attendant with a lovely face looks tired.

For a few seconds, it doesn't occur to Ulrike to reply. With some delay, she answers, "Thank you." She's already passed the attendant and has to turn to address her. But the woman's eyes are no longer on Ulrike.

She steps into the jetway.

She's taken a series of English courses and found a few Americans to practice conversation. She feels ready for this new country. *Except most things people say are incomprehensible, marred by slurring and mumbling.* She's in a vast, excessively air-conditioned space filled with people. Ulrike reaches into her backpack for a sweater on what, through the window, looks like a hot summer day.

As she scans the terminal for Luggage Pickup, Ulrike reaffirms something that has made her feel optimistic all day since the long customs line at JFK. *Black faces, Latino faces, Asian faces, all kinds of faces I can't classify. How delightful. I'm in the presence of a multiplicity I've never encountered outside a movie or TV screen.*

Boarding in Frankfurt, she worried about the logistics of her travels and the rest of her life in a new country. Today, her worries have retreated; she's filled with joy. *So this is America? All sorts of different, interesting, beautiful characters. All these colors, after two decades among the GDR's pale shadows.* As Ulrike makes her way through the boarding area, a sign depicting a white rectangle with a handle confirms that she's on the right track.

Her classes at Berkeley start in two weeks. She doesn't know where Berkeley is, but she's heard the name. *It's okay. I'll find it. It's accessible by metro. Metro has a funny name here. What is it now?*

How lovely to be out in the real world. The world uninfected by the communist virus, uncompromised by ideology, untouched by post-reunification conflicts.

The land where the former Stasi don't exist.

1991, BERKELEY

Ulrike walks east along University Avenue. The Berkeley campus with its good-looking Campanile awaits ahead, its architecture more European than she'd expected. She crosses Shattuck and scans the area, trying to choose between a cappuccino at Café Roma on her left and an actual lunch. *Am I hungry enough?* The diversity of food choices still strikes her as a bizarre fortune. Not enough time has passed since reunification; capitalism has yet to fully penetrate East Germany.

Her stomach rumbles as if in answer to her question. *Lunch it is.* She smiles as she walks. *Will people wonder why I'm smiling?* No one seems to care. Relaxed faces are typical here. She reaches the end of University Avenue where it runs into the campus. Green bushes and neat paths between pristine buildings, the entire setup animated by hundreds of running, walking, sitting, and thinking young people. Students.

Now she's one of them.

How strange that feels.

I'm not in prison anymore.

A burger joint. Mexican food. Several Indian restaurants. Indian, a cuisine she's never tried. Viceroy is right behind her, and The Taste of India's sign hangs on the street corner to her right. Ulrike walks over and looks in. The large dining room occupies the entire corner of the building. *I might regret it, but I think I'll love it.*

She enters.

Barely anyone seems to be an ethnic Indian, which only goes to show: nationality is a fucked up concept. Void of meaning. The host hands her a menu and fills her water glass. She's not used to restaurants. The menu is long, and nothing on it is familiar. She can identify the categories: lamb, curry, bread, chicken.

Tandoori chicken?

Sounds like a good choice.

She also orders an Indian beer, Taj Mahal. She'd never tried a beer that wasn't German. *I'm farther away from the Stasi world than I've ever been. What a fucking relief.*

The beer arrives, the beautiful white building on the label. Ulrike takes a sip. *A good pilsner.* Through the window on her left, the campus floats its ever-shifting promise. *Young people moving about unimpeded—what could be more life-affirming? To be an intellectual and an artist here, in the free world—is that even possible? I never expected communism to perish so quickly.* She wants to stuff a dinner candle up Honecker's ass, but that might be a waste of a candle.

A young man in a red T-shirt walks in and scans the dining area. *Seeking familiar faces?* He is good-looking and somehow heroic, his dark hair long, his brown eyes unafraid of the world.

"Are you new here?" Before Ulrike has noticed, the young man is sitting in her booth opposite her.

"I came to the United States a week ago." She feels embarrassed. "How did you know?"

An attentive expression on the dude's face slowly shifts to hilarity. "I meant here, this restaurant. I had no idea you were an immigrant. But that's nothing unusual here."

Is this what I am? An immigrant?

Am I going to stay here after school?

Hell, yes.

Ulrike laughs. "Sorry, it's new to me, this whole thing. Speaking English. Speaking freely. All of it."

"Where are you from?"

The conversation is easy, even if it takes Ulrike two or three tries to understand some of the American idioms. Her meal arrives.

"And you?" She asks the young man. "Did you order?"

"Not yet."

Ulrike has been horny like hell since she broke up with her latest boyfriend back in Dresden more than three months ago. *But I can't just wrap my legs around the first American man who expresses an interest.* He orders, and they eat and talk. The spicy chicken burns Ulrike's mouth, bringing tears to her eyes.

"Can I call you?" he asks when they are done with their lunch.

"I don't have a phone number yet."

"I'll give you mine." He scribbles a number on the customer's copy of his receipt.

"Thank you." Ulrike stashes the receipt away in a small pocket in her wallet, empty until now.

Will I call?

I don't have a clue, but it's good to have someone I can call.

2003, BERKELEY

A train passes, and the BART station is empty again as Ulrike stares into the tunnel.

"We worked with West German colleagues in the '80s," David says. "Lovely people. That was a tense time, I can tell you. How was it for you?"

"My father was at *Hohenschönhausen*, the Stasi prison in Berlin. You must have heard about it. My mother turned into a zombie. The Stasi kept after our family for years. And then, the whole thing just stopped. Most people here can't relate to any of that. It's like pressure inside your head all your life, and then the pressure is removed. It turns into a reverse pressure, as if your head is about to explode from a lack of concern, from all the options and freedoms. I'm not describing it right. It wasn't a terrific way to spend your childhood, that's for sure."

"What did they get your father for?"

"Helping people escape to the West. Specifically, this activist, Otto Bauer. Bauer was the one who sealed it for the Stasi. Bigger fish, as you say here. They were determined to nail anyone who'd helped him."

"I met Otto Bauer in Frankfurt in '87 or '88. A good man. Your father did the world a real service."

"You're kidding, right?" *I'm not six anymore. I can tell when my leg is being pulled, especially if it's pulled so hard it's about to be torn off.*

"I wouldn't joke about something like this. Otto was a great guy. He died a few years ago."

What am I supposed to make of the fact that Otto Bauer, a person I've never met, is no longer alive? Nothing, nothing at all— and if it's nothing, why do I feel moved? I should ask Papa about this.

Another San Francisco train stops, the doors open—but Ulrike is not tempted. Something about this conversation keeps a hold on her—perhaps David himself, disheveled, tired, but still elegant in his simple clothes. *Unthreatening for a spy—not Vogel's intimidating figure, but a kind, unassuming type, here to protect the world from those like Vogel. Naïve as fuck, but that's how it feels.*

There's something else to this, some bitterness in David's response, in his face, prompting Ulrike to focus on his urgency, "And you? What about you?"

"I may be in trouble, and I may deserve it." David's face is thoughtful.

In a leap of faith or emotion, Ulrike accepts that this man indeed knew Otto Bauer. That this man is in danger.

"Why do you deserve it?"

"Because not everything I've done ended up being a good thing."

"Isn't that true of everyone?" *Most things I've done ended up harmful.*

"Is it?" David shrugs. "I don't know."

"I've never told anyone before..." Ulrike pauses, knowing she will say it, lingering on this side of it. She is happy to be able to tell, finally.

"Yes?" David's eyes retain their openness.

"I betrayed my father. I signed."

"You signed?" David's voice is neutral as he looks past her into the empty BART tunnel.

He knows what I mean.

"I signed a statement confirming that my father was smuggling people across the border. I had to." Ulrike sighs. "I thought I had to."

"Why?"

"The Stasi had stuff on my mother too. Vogel told me my dad was already doomed. They had plenty of evidence. He was going to put my mother away as well if I didn't cooperate."

"I see."

A loud voice announces the next train, but Ulrike lets the sound slide by without hearing it. David's response was so neutral she feels the need to elaborate.

"I resisted for the longest time, but he just kept showing up. He had this nasty tactic, parking by my school, of all places. That way, everyone noticed him. What a creep. I still have nightmares about him." Ulrike recalls the recurring dream, the dreadful scene in the car with Vogel. In the dream, she feels as if she forgot the right answer, the smart way out—and now, she and her family are doomed. "He showed me photos of my mother and father and this Otto Bauer—at least, that's who the person was supposed to be. If both my parents went to prison, I would go to a children's home. If they wanted to make a point, it could be a place like Torgau. Essentially, a youth punishment camp. Look it up." Ulrike's hands are sweating. She wipes them on her jeans, but that doesn't help. "I gave up my father instead of giving up both parents and my own future."

"I see," David repeats.

Is that a technique to encourage the interlocutor to go on? In any case, she's in a talkative mood.

"I often ask myself if I had the right. And what comes up every time is that I didn't. I can't help wondering: if my father's case was so solid, why did they need my signature in the first place?"

These days, Papa seems to be okay, more than okay, but Ulrike has read all about the way political prisoners were treated. One detail won't leave her mind: they were forced to sleep on their backs only. Ostensibly so the guards could see their hands. Turn in your sleep—and you're awoken and forced to adjust. Ulrike has never dared to ask her father if he's learned to sleep in a different position again.

"This must be why my life is so fucked," she says. "I made my father pay the price for our entire family, and he doesn't even know. I'm afraid to tell him. He'll hate me forever."

What if Papa does know? And if he doesn't, he might request his Stasi file and find out. Since 1992, everyone has the right to see their record if one exists.

"He'll understand." David nods a few times.

"How do you know?"

"I have a daughter too. I'd forgive her. It sounds like your testimony wasn't really necessary—just something for this Vogel character to seal the deal with himself and the system and to get an extra credit with his boss."

Is that true? How can I know? Was I a pawn who made no difference rather than a black queen who sent her father to prison? Can my guilt be so easily absolved?

"Thanks for saying so. How old is your daughter?"

"About your age."

"What's her name?"

Briefly, David seems to consider something. "Ruth."

"Ruth," Ulrike repeats, holding this small, pleasing sound on her tongue. "A lovely name. Tell me about her."

"She's a chemist." David pauses and stares into the tunnel. "It's hard for me to tell, but I don't think she's happy."

"No one is happy."

David ponders this for a while. "No, I suppose not. I was worried I might have gotten them into trouble. Ruth and my wife. Made them vulnerable. But now I have a solution."

"Good. Why would they be in trouble?"

"Let's say there is some information I don't want to share with my colleagues. I don't need to tell you any more. I've destroyed those documents, you see? I'll tell my colleague and be done with it."

"Will you be safe?"

"Someone like me doesn't deserve to be safe if you know what I mean."

A light in Ulrike's head—she feels tuned in, present in the moment of an essential truth. She tears up. "I feel the same way. I feel that my life, the pure, real thing of it, was extinguished back then when I signed that paper. It may have been extinguished the moment the Stasi first spoke to me. Or even the moment I was born in that fucked up corrupt land. Now, it's just half of me living on." Goose pimples on her skin, a cold glow in her head. *This statement has brought me closer than ever to an understanding of my own life.* And with that, the moment breaks like a sheet of glass: it's not an intense conversation anymore; it's her life. *The same as it always is, the fucked up mess of it.*

David just stares, his eyes sad, defeated. The strangeness of this situation descends upon Ulrike in a massive wave of confusion and apprehension. *Who is this guy, anyway? Is he putting me on?* She glances at her watch: it's past noon. *We've been talking for over an hour. I'm late as doomsday.*

As if in an answer, another train's roar grows in the tunnel.

"I have to go," she says apologetically.

"Of course you do."

The train pulls up to the platform, and Ulrike stares at its approaching face instead of making eye contact. She feels guilty, as if, somehow, she had mistreated David—even though she just met him. *It's not David I've wronged.*

The train slows.

"Good luck today," Ulrike says.

"Remember not to turn around." David points over her shoulder, where the camera must be.

CHAPTER TWENTY-NINE

2003

It was a difficult night. Ruth kept waking. *Reading Ulrike's client's book before bed may not have been the best idea.* Something he'd written was sticking in Ruth's mind.

> When my wife left, I was sad at first, no doubt. A month or two later, I realized I was happy, so happy! This happened unexpectedly. I'd had no idea. I felt guilty and relieved.

To kill himself right before Ulrike's eyes? An unimaginable spectacle to enact on another human being. How can a person who does something like this write a book worth reading? What does Peter think of all of this?

The clock next to her bed showed 2:13 a.m. Ruth made herself a cup of chamomile tea, hoping for a soporific effect. The drink lacked coffee's pleasant bitterness.

She tried to sleep. She wished Peter would call back, but the three days of silence since her third voice mail confirmed that their brief fling was over. *And for the best. This whole Ulrike obsession is an unhealthy thing, something I have to leave behind.*

She was uncomfortable in her bed—now cold, now sweating. She opened the window, closed it again. The street lay heavy with fog. The ocean breathed in the darkness. Hopeless against the future, the dramatic dark silhouette of the Golden Gate Park's windmill waited amid the trees.

The doorbell rang. Ruth turned in bed and checked the alarm clock.

2:16 am.

Who can it be?

Peter?

No, no, he doesn't have my address.

Ruth leaped out of bed, hastily threw her bathrobe on, and ran downstairs. She pushed the door open.

It wasn't Peter.

Two cops waited outside the gate, their figures casting long, ominous shadows in the streetlight's glare.

"Miss Hanson?"

"Yes." She squinted to better read the expressions on their faces.

Not enough light.

"I'm Officer Lee; this is Officer Henrickson. We're from the Medical Examiner's Office."

"What...what happened?"

"Miss Hanson, do you mind if we talk inside?"

"Yes, of course. I mean...I don't. I don't mind." With shaking hands, Ruth unlocked the gate, pushed it open.

"Thank you."

The two followed her in. Ruth was grateful for the delay. She could already tell that the news wasn't going to be good.

Mother?

What did she do now?

"Please have a seat." She pointed at the chairs surrounding the dining room table.

Neither seemed inclined to sit down.

"Miss Hanson." Why did Officer Lee keep repeating her name? "I'm afraid we have bad news. There's been a fire. A fire at your mother's house. Your mother...she was inside."

"Inside? How is...where is she?"

"I'm so sorry, but your mother didn't make it."

Is this really happening?

"She didn't make it?"

"I'm afraid not."

So that was it. Her mother, no longer present in this world, so soon after her father's death, and Ulrike's.

This is too much, way too much.

What does Ulrike have to do with any of this? She isn't family, not even someone I knew. How mixed up everything has become. The next image in Ruth's head was of a burning cigarette in her mother's mouth. Linda had been dancing on the brink of danger, yet Ruth did nothing.

"Miss Hanson, are you okay?" The second officer's eyes were kind and attentive. Already, his last name had escaped her memory.

"Yes," she replied, as if from somewhere else. "I'll be okay. And the house? How's the house?" She regretted the question; it might have sounded insensitive. But she wanted to know.

"There's significant damage, but we're not really equipped to comment on that, sorry."

"Of course."

"Is there anything we can help you with? Can we contact someone for you? Get you something?"

"No, no, thank you." Ruth shivered. "I'll be okay."

Do these two deal with sobbing and screaming every day? Proba-

bly. By contrast, Ruth felt muted, almost frozen, her emotional capacity overloaded.

"Thank you," she said again. "Thank you for coming to tell me."

When the coroners left, she sat in the corner of her bed, lost as to what to do next. The clock said 2:42. She felt like a molecule subjected to an undisclosed reaction, observed by curious eyes she, herself, couldn't see. She desperately needed someone, someone to feel bad for her.

Is anyone out there, at all?

Peter, oh Peter.

Then she remembered. His mobile phone. Ruth's hands shook as she riffled through her purse for Peter's business card. She found it, a neutral green like his company logo. With a rapidly beating heart and a deafening buzz in her head, Ruth counted to ten, then dialed, expecting an answering machine. *Do mobile phones even have such a feature?*

"Hello." Peter's voice.

She'd missed that voice. Breath caught in her throat. She'd never known this could happen literally.

"Peter, oh Peter. It's Ruth. My mother...oh no...I'm sorry." She constrained herself, forced her voice into a more controlled range. "There's been a fire, but that's hardly your business now, is it?" She felt embarrassed.

"Oh my god. What happened?"

"A fire at my parents' house. My mom, she..." Ruth couldn't finish.

"Ruth, I'm so sorry. Do you want me to come?"

"I...wasn't expecting you to answer." Ruth didn't know how to best express the perplexing mix of emotions and wishes spiraling out of control inside her. Her hand with Peter's business card kept shaking; she tossed the card onto the bed next to her.

"I'm so sorry I didn't return your calls," Peter said. "I really enjoyed the other night. Really. It was special. Then I felt guilty because of Ulrike. But after thinking about it some more, I don't see why I should be guilty. It's not like I'm cheating on her."

He was silent for a few seconds. Ruth, too, was at a loss for words.

"Do you want me to come?" Peter asked again.

"Please." She was crying. "Please."

Ruth focused and recited her address.

"I'm on my way," Peter said.

* * *

Ruth was undone by the time Peter arrived. She sobbed as he held her.

"Let's go inside," she finally said.

"I'm so sorry." Tears in Peter's eyes.

"It's all my fault."

"Your fault? Why?" Peter's brows converged uncomprehendingly, but it looked like a kind surprise; Ruth didn't feel alienated.

"I've been too preoccupied with my own fears and challenges. My dad's death. Mom was unraveling, and I did nothing. I just kept fighting with her, giving her a tough time. I should have checked her into a rehab."

"Would she have allowed that?" Peter's careful, attentive eyes.

Ruth hadn't considered that. *Of course not.*

"So you don't think it's my fault?" She longed to be absolved by this man, who had nothing to do with her mother's death or her parents' problems. But he'd also lost someone close. She wanted his forgiveness viscerally.

"Of course not. How can it be your fault?"

Ruth didn't have an answer. Peter's words lingered in her head. They made sense, yet she knew her guilt would not be assuaged so easily. *My parents are gone. Ulrike is gone. What the fuck am I supposed to do with my life?*

At least she had things to take care of. Things to keep her distracted. Funeral arrangements. An insurance adjuster was probably going to call her in the morning. *Is it the adjuster who calls first?* She didn't know.

I'll find out, soon.

* * *

Ruth could still smell the fire. She stood by the ruins of the Russian Hill house. The black remnants of the roof lay amid burned wood and misshapen metal. Ruth could swear the ruins were still emitting smoke, but of course, they weren't.

She had already taken care of the logistics; the building crew were here to take measurements. The insurance would cover most of the rebuilding. The investigators were unable to determine where exactly the fire had started. For the hundredth time, Ruth imagined her mother upstairs. A cigarette burning on the bed next to her. The sheet catching fire. *She probably died from asphyxiation. But if the fire started in her bed, she'd feel the heat first. Wouldn't she run downstairs?* These circular thoughts wouldn't leave Ruth's mind. She imagined her mother's body, lifeless, slowly catching fire, like a slab of wood. She imagined that body falling through the floor to land in the fire below. *No, no.* Ruth chased these thoughts away.

She remembered her last conversation with her mother, Linda's drunk abandon. *If only I'd done something.* The second floor had collapsed, but the walls of the first floor remained, charred, freed of any content they were intended to protect. Ruth had no choice but to get used to this uncertainty. Too many questions about her parents' deaths remained. *I better get used to them. They will never be answered, now.*

2004

Ruth stood at the north end of one of the vast cemeteries in Colma, the place where most of San Francisco's dead were buried. *More dead here than the living.* Ulrike stared back from the gravestone, a confident and defiant expression on her beautiful face.

"Ulrike Schumacher, 1970-2003," the inscription read.

That was all.

Rows of gravestones covered the green grass all around her. Small hills hovered in the distance. Peter had selected this place. Peter loved everything green.

That man really made sense to Ruth, with his perfectionism and his dedication to the environment, his goofy sense of humor. And it seemed as if Ruth made sense to Peter. They had grown to enjoy each other, perhaps too much for the circumstances that had connected them. Still, Ruth preferred to visit Ulrike on her own. It was cleaner that way. A more honest conversation.

"They reclassified my dad's murder as homicide, you know. I hate my dad. I miss him too. His secrets must have caught up with him. I'm beginning to think they'll never find his killers."

Ulrike didn't reply.

"I can't believe it's been nearly a year since you died. It feels both longer and shorter. My whole life feels like someone else's. Like yours, maybe." Ruth shrugged. "Human affairs are so strange, don't you think? Totally unlike science."

Ulrike might say, *Why the fuck did you steal my husband? My life? What the fuck are you doing here?* Instead, Ulrike said nothing as Ruth stood over her, torn about her reasons for being there.

"I'm pregnant, you know." She felt tears roll down her face. "Do you mind? Peter told me you never wanted children."

All she knew was Peter's version of the story. *What would Ulrike say about this?*

"I haven't told Peter yet," Ruth added. "I was thinking, Ulrike or Ulrich would be a great middle name. Don't you think? I'm getting way ahead of myself, I know. Peter might not like the idea."

Ulrike was at the root of their shared life, every day, for as long as the two of them stayed together. If not for Ulrike, this thing Peter and Ruth had—this thing that was developing between them— would not have happened.

Ruth's chest tightened from the finality of Ulrike's disappearance. That beautiful, intelligent, unique person didn't exist anymore, not as a physical entity nor a brain capable of thought. Instead, her broken body lay here under Ruth's feet. Ruth missed her more than either of her parents.

"How can you be so gone, yet so present?"

CHAPTER THIRTY

Ulrike squints. The sun is still bright as it hovers at mid-height, getting ready to give up for the day. She and Peter sit at their small kitchen table. Ulrike has been trying to have a conversation, but Peter is excited about his newfangled cellphone, like a puppy with its teeth on a chewy toy. He has brought a couple of these from work and hands one to Ulrike. She's been reluctant to use a cellphone so far—too much contact, like committing to be perpetually available to everyone who might want to reach her.

It's an unusual day. Peter took Friday afternoon off, just for the hell of it. The two of them have made no plans. It's just past four.

"Go ahead and activate it." Peter grins. "We can call each other."

"Activate?"

"Just a couple of steps you have to follow to connect to the network."

"Is this something they might use to track us?"

"No. Well, maybe. Good question." For a moment, Peter looks puzzled. "Why would anyone want to track us?"

David Conrad may have the answer. What a strange guy. Surely he must be some writer on drugs or a mental patient off his prescription. Both categories are prominent in this crazy ass metropolis.

"They wouldn't, would they?" Ulrike is tempted to add something sarcastic, but she forces herself onto a kinder path and extends her hand for the gadget. "What do I do?"

Something incongruent in David Conrad's act. His concern for his daughter? What was her name? Her father is full of secrets that may blow up in everyone's face. For a moment, Ulrike is concerned for that young woman she doesn't know, whose predicament draws her in, drags her out of her smartass indifference. *I'd like to warn her if I could reach her.*

"Just turn it on and call my number," Peter says. "It's already programmed in."

"Sounds easy enough."

So typical, Peter and his electronic toys. He's already working on his own identical gadget, the manual before him like an exciting puzzle. *What the fuck.* She was hoping to talk about Brigita's invitation. Ulrike hesitates and watches Peter play with the buttons. *What was it I forgot to ask David?* She smiles as she remembers his semi-disheveled presentation, his unthinkable pronouncements.

"I met the strangest person last week," she says when Peter appears to be done. "You're not going to believe it."

"Sorry, Uli. Can I just finish this?" Peter's eyes glance up at her, but he doesn't await confirmation before diving back into his tinkering.

"I thought you *were* finished."

"I will be, in a minute."

Ulrike holds herself still and takes a breath. *Sally and I have worked this through.* "No problem," she says. "Would you mind setting up mine too? You're so good at these things. It would take me an hour and a half to figure it out."

Peter fumbles with the small object. *He is beautiful as a god—how is that not enough? Nothing makes sense, nothing.*

His face lightens. *Success.* He puts his unit aside and picks up Ulrike's. Confidently, he repeats the steps. A minute later, he hands the silvery thing to her, a kindly smile on his face as if he'd just done her a grand favor.

"Thank you," Ulrike says.

"No problem. I'll give you a call." Peter scrutinizes the tiny keyboard, the humor of calling someone in the same room eluding him.

Ulrike waits.

The item in her own hand begins to ring and vibrate like a mad bug. She flips it open and presses Accept. Peter's voice is both in the room and inside the small thing, a sinister metaphor for authority. Vogel might use a trick like this. Ulrike reminds herself not to react negatively. *It's not Peter's fault. He wasn't born in the GDR; he couldn't have predicted my reaction.*

"Hello," Peter says.

"Hi, Peter."

"I love you," he says.

She hesitates just a little.

"I love you too." She glances at him inquiringly to determine whether this charade is over. *I wish we could move on with our evening.* But Peter stares somewhere at an angle from her, in a direction where nothing appears to be. She flips her shiny square of nonsense closed and puts it away in her jeans' pocket.

"Wait, can you try calling me back first?" Peter says. "Just to make sure."

"Shit, Peter. I've been waiting forever to talk to you. Can you just give me five minutes of conversation before we go back to playing walkie-talkie?"

"Sorry, Uli. I thought this was fun." Coldness seeps into Peter's voice.

Fun? Peter's defensiveness annoys her, so she takes a leap. "I want to move to Berlin. Please move to Berlin with me." Right away, she knows this came out too abrupt, like a crabby whim rather than an essential need.

Is it?

For a few seconds, Peter just stares. "Berlin? Why Berlin?"

"You know why. I'm not making ends meet here in San Francisco. Life would be easier for both of us. You have a great resume— you could get a similar job. A better one. I could land something meaningful. And we could buy a flat and pay half our rent here."

"But it's not all about money. I'm in the middle of so many things." Peter looks puzzled. "My family is here. I can't just leave them."

"Don't you see what's happening to me?"

It's clear as fuck that most things happening to me are not Peter's fault, but it's so easy to blame him. So easy.

"I do. But I can't just run off to another country because you're having difficulties." Peter looks irritated. "There must be another way."

"Can you please consider it? Can we at least go check it out?"

"How?" Peter's arms are up in the air. *He's so full of himself.* "We don't have the money to go check out Berlin."

True. The fucking money is not there, and it's my fault, as usual. This conversation is not going anywhere. It won't work out, after all, the whole thing, me and Peter, me and San Francisco, me and this whole setup. All energy leaks away from her, replaced by anger.

"I need some air." Ulrike rises from the table.

With surprise, she watches herself act decisive. *How American of me, 'I need some air.'* She grabs her new red purse and makes straight for the door, her steps measured and deliberate like an ant's, except she doesn't have to carry dead weight on her back.

What was it William wrote?

When my wife left, I was sad at first, no doubt. A month or two later, I realized I was happy, so happy! This happened unexpectedly. I'd had no idea. I felt guilty and relieved.

So different from the way he talked about it. The memory of William's suicide makes Ulrike shiver. *Is this how Peter is going to feel once I'm out of his life? Will he find a quick replacement?* She'll take Brigita up on her offer. This choice is as clear now as it was impossible a few days ago.

Ulrike walks to her car. The day is warm for February. The windshield is covered with raindrops. The VW bug is a friendly thing—ironic, considering she's just decided to move back to the country of its origin. *Where exactly in Germany do they make these things? Must be someplace in the former West.* She is going to Berlin, and yet she can never forgive its past.

In the car, something is off—something awkward in her pocket. *The cellphone.* She twists uncomfortably to pull it out and drops it in the dead space near the radio. A small light on the gadget blinks green. *How fucking optimistic.* The tool keeps reminding her of Vogel. The last time she saw him, in '88, he was as threatening as ever—but somehow, Ulrike was less scared. And then, Vogel just disappeared. She never saw him again.

Contrary to all expectations, the former Stasi were allowed to resume normal lives. *I hope they were crippled by what they had done. I hope they are impotent, incapable of happiness.* But she also knows that to be a Stasi, one would have already abdicated conscience. *In a better world, there would have been a price to pay.*

She's driving South on Van Ness. The city is as busy as ever. *It's a juicy city, I must admit.* The events of the past days are mixed in her head. She is more excited than sad. She takes a right on

Market. *Luckily, it's all coming to an end. This marriage thing I have with Peter is over. He will never agree to come along, and I have no right to pressure him. It's been nice and it's given much to both of us, but there's not enough to go on, not enough common future, common interest, common anything. Not enough care left—in me, at any rate. What a lovely man, Peter—I'll miss him terribly, and yet, stopping here must be good for him, too. It's a good point for both of us. One we can recover from.*

Ulrike takes a right on 17th and heads West until she's on Stanyan. From here, only a right turn makes sense; the area on the left is nothing but confusing passages leading nowhere. *Now I know where I'm headed.* A minute later, Golden Gate Park appears on her left. Young men in hoodies hang about selling pot and acid. A small drum circle exerts itself on the grass.

Peter will meet someone who can appreciate him, share his technical interests and his optimism. Someone he deserves. Someone who won't cheat on him. Ulrike finds herself smiling thinking of this. The traffic is moderate; the sky has turned gray with an occasional intrusion of the sun. *I'll miss these beautiful small mansions, this ever changing light, this airy architecture. I'll miss the hills.*

And where is David Conrad now?

For some reason, David's lost face is stuck in her mind.

Hopefully, back on his meds.

The traffic stalls at Park Presidio, but Ulrike is in no rush. Golden Gate Park is long and lovely on her left. A blue Honda turns a corner and hovers in front of Ulrike's car, moving much slower than the speed limit. *What a pain in the ass, unusual for this over-caffeinated city.* Luckily, the ocean should be right there, just ahead—as indeed it is when the Honda makes a right. The old windmill's optimistic wings float on the left.

Yes, of course. The ocean. Ulrike takes a right on Great Highway. Visiting Cliff House is a proper way to say goodbye to San Francisco. She's not leaving immediately—in fact, it might take months—but the choice is firm, material inside her. The cellphone begins to ring and vibrate and dance in its spot by the radio. *It must be Peter. What does he want?*

Never mind. I'll deal with it later. Should have turned it off. The thing keeps buzzing and shaking, inviting Ulrike into a crazy computerized future she's not ready for. *Poor Peter—may he have his future and his cellphone and his wonderful life in this wonderful city, without me.*

The curve of the road follows the pattern of the hills on Ulrike's right. *Cliff House will appear in sight any moment.*

But what is it over there? Something red.

Ulrike strains her eyes.

A red spot on the green slope on her right.

A person.

A woman.

As Ulrike gets closer, she confirms: yes, a woman, tall, her hair blond like Ulrike's, but much longer. *Her red coat is extreme, exuberant, a challenge to anyone who thinks our lives have run out of passion, meaning, future.* The ocean's gray mass dances on Ulrike's left, past the rows of cars parked next to Cliff House. The woman's hair is wild in the wind.

Ulrike inhales. Exhales.

Now the woman on the slope is close. *She is magic. I wish I'd brought my camera. How was I supposed to know I'd have a fight with Peter, go out driving, end up here? There's no need for the camera. The image is so perfect I'll remember it for the rest of my life.* The ocean's indifference on the left and the woman's vibrant presence. *Like a fairy tale, Red Riding Something or Other.*

This will be my first painting. It will look good in oil. The ocean always looks good in oil, and red always looks good everywhere. The woman's face is beautiful, even if Ulrike can't see it quite clearly yet.

What is it about her? Some tension. Someone honks, but Ulrike ignores it. *Soon, I will be done with all these obnoxious San Francisco drivers.* The silver thing next to the radio keeps ringing, vibrating, ringing, vibrating, a dying animal that won't die. Ulrike squints to see clearer. She's getting close fast. *What is it about the woman's face, her expression—what makes it so urgent, so beautiful?* Ulrike cranes her neck and tilts her head up to get a clearer view.

Now, she can see.

It's an expression of concern.

Yes, concern

ACKNOWLEDGMENTS

With gratitude to Laurie Stahman for German thoughts, words and connections, and for sharing this life of reading and thinking.

Special thanks to Uli Irmler for her historical and cultural input and the book/film suggestions, and for the use of her first name.

Special thanks to Michael Keefe for his full manuscript review and other contributions.

Thanks to Lindsay Hill for reminding me of the Brezhnev/Honecker kiss and to Darlene Pagán for sharing the Marie Curie quote. Thanks to Christian Petzold for letting the broader public know about Torgau in his film "Barbara."

Thanks to Saoirse Grey for her help with imagining a chemist's workspace.

With endless gratitude to fellow Guttery members for their reviewes: Joseph Ahearne, Melanie Alldritt, Mo Daviau, Susan DeFreitas, Michael Keefe, Cody Luff, Tracy Manaster, Lois Medina, Lara Messersmith-Glavin, Margaret Pinard, Tammy Lynne Stoner, Jamie Yourdon.

Many thanks to everyone at Running Wild, especially Lisa Kastner, Evangeline Estropia, and Emir Orucevic.

Special thanks to my editor, Rod Giley, for helping whip this book into a better shape.

I'm grateful to my agent, Laura Strachan, for all her effort on my behalf.

RESOURCES

- Anna Funder, "Stasiland: Stories from Behind the Berlin Wall", Harper Perennial 2011
- Hester Vaizey, "Born in the GDR", Oxford University Press 2014
- Gary Bruce "The Firm – The Inside Story of the Stasi", Oxford University Press 2010
- Georg C. Bertsch, Ernst Hedler "SED – Stunning Eastern Design", Taschen 1994
- David Heather "DDR Posters", Prestel 2014
- The Baltic Initiative And Network, http://coldwarsites.net/country/germany/closed-juvenile-detention-centre
- The Telegraph, http://www.telegraph.co.uk/comment/personal-view/7903324/How-I-survived-an-East-German-prison.html
- Daily Mail, http://www.dailymail.co.uk/news/article-2235213/Cold-stark-images-Berlins-Stasi-prison-scene-unimaginable-horrors.html

- Wired, https://www.wired.com/2010/10/phillip-lohoefener/

ABOUT RUNNING WILD PRESS

Running Wild Press publishes stories that cross genres with great stories and writing. RIZE publishes great genre stories written by people of color and by authors who identify with other marginalized groups. Our team consists of:

Lisa Diane Kastner, Founder and Executive Editor
Joelle Mitchell, Licensing and Strategy Lead
Cody Sisco, Acquisition Editor, RIZE
Benjamin White, Acquisition Editor, Running Wild
Peter A. Wright, Acquisition Editor, Running Wild
Resa Alboher, Editor
Angela Andrews, Editor
Sandra Bush, Editor
Ashley Crantas, Editor
Rebecca Dimyan, Editor
Abigail Efird, Editor
Aimee Hardy, Editor
Henry L. Herz, Editor
Cecilia Kennedy, Editor

ABOUT RUNNING WILD PRESS

Barbara Lockwood, Editor
AE Williams, Editor
Scott Schultz, Editor
Rod Gilley, Editor

Evangeline Estropia, Product Manager
Kimberly Ligutan, Product Manager
Pulp Art Studios, Cover Design
Standout Books, Interior Design
Polgarus Studios, Interior Design

Learn more about us and our stories at www.runningwildpress.com

Loved these stories and want more? Follow us at runningwildpublishing.com, www.facebook.com/runningwild-press, on Twitter @lisadkastner @RunWildBooks